LORDE

THE BIOGRAPHY

by Marc Shapiro

OMNIBUS PRESS

London / New York / Paris / Sydney / Copenhagen / Berlin / Madrid / Tokyo

ACKNOWLEDGMENTS

Nancy Shapiro, my wife and love, forever and always.

My daughter, Rachael.

My granddaughter Lily.

My agent, Lori Perkins.

Riverdale Avenue Books, which continues to fight the good fight.

Mike, Brady, Fitch.

The great authors. The great musicians. The great artists.

And finally to Lorde. True uncompromising intelligence does not come along too often. We should fully embrace it when it does.

TABLE OF CONTENTS

LORDE CAN READ

Stop the Presses! Most of the reigning pop music idols in recent memory would have trouble spelling pop.

Trust me, I'm not quick on the trigger when it comes to slamming easy targets. But after penning two books on Justin Bieber and following the exploits of a bunch of people named Katy, Selena and some blokes named One Direction, I think it is safe to say that these people are not rocket scientists, and that their level of talent and charisma makes them ideally suited for the teen idol circuit.

But candidates for *Mensa*? I don't think so.

Don't get me wrong. These pop stars are very good at taking orders. Hand them a pre fab song and, to a person, they'll sing it, no problem. Put them on tour and they'll respond by entertaining the masses in a high tech, polished, superficial way. Give them some sanitized talking points to toss out to the press and they're all over it. But an original thought, opinion or even an ounce of enticing creativity? Don't bet the farm on that one. Puppets on a string? The perceptive Eight Ball says yes. But this is the generation that is perceived as having a short attention span and being blandly superficial. So who's to argue with the easy way out?

All of which brings me to the fact that writing a book

about Lorde is such a joy. Because Lorde, quite simply, is smart. Book smart as opposed to street smart. Yes, I realize the former is a dying skill set and the latter is the order of the day, Lorde is decidedly the exception.

There are no easy answers when it comes to this seventeen-year-old wunderkind. Her worldview does not allow for anything less than inquiring and persisting. Lorde may not have all the answers but she puts up a fairly convincing argument that she does.

For openers she read books. Books without pictures. Real adult books. Books your parents most likely read. In fact, she reportedly had read over a thousand of them, by authors such as Raymond Carver, Sylvia Plath and J.D. Salinger, all by the time she was twelve. Lorde can talk philosophical and sociological issues until the cows come home.

Her much publicized take on feminism is quick and easy and, most of all, makes sense. And at the end it will make cold, logical sense. If you want to know what real feminism is all about in 2014, forget Gloria Steinem. Just ask Lorde.

This seventeen-year-old is wise beyond her years when it comes to that decades old philosophy. And when she was administered IQ tests at the ripe old age of six, the consensus was that she was six going on twenty-one. She was writing short stories long before she could chronologically qualify as a teen.

Lorde was looking at the world in an honest, intellectual way before she was a teen. You've got to love it.

And so it is more than a little surprising to discover that at a time when she could easily qualify for a master's program at any major university, she has chosen to put that future aside, in favor of becoming the biggest pop star on the planet.

And yes, readers. She can spell pop.

Lorde writes lyrics the way she thinks. She could easily write boy meets girl radio- friendly product but has chosen her own way, an often contemplative, borderline high-brow way of looking at teen angst and day-to-day life of those who traditionally appear rootless. It is a style that is deep, very inward-looking but one that, when combined with melodies and choruses, is very familiar to the modern/progressive/ fringe music movement.

Lorde waves her flag of independence high. She revels in the fact that she writes her own songs, controls what goes on behind the scenes in the business side of the music business, and regularly does verbal battle with people twice her age, and still comes out smelling like a rose.

Let's face it, to wear a Cramps T-shirt for a *Rolling Stone* cover shoot is the height of independence. No, Lorde is not a perfect creation. But then what would you expect from a seventeen year old? She has been known to be spontaneous to the point where independence blurs over into asinine behavior. But she is smart enough to realize that being very young and being an ass just comes with the territory . . . Before she moves on and makes up for it with something insightful and smart.

Lorde is anti-pop in the best possible way. She speaks her mind rather than mouthing public relations platitudes and is not afraid to air those opinions and convictions. And if somebody gets hit by her intellectual fallout, well that's too bad.

This young woman is just too smart and honest for words. She not afraid to take shots at her pop music peers and has done so with regularity. Occasionally she has backtracked on such attacks but has even couched those "missteps" in a coat of logic and reality that would have most people think she was actually right the first time.

Her life and approach is minimalist, from her Goth/Thrift Store chic she wears both on and offstage to the hypnotic way she moves in concert. It's all so inventive and free-thinking. It almost seems too good to be true.

Lorde still lives at home. She actually likes her parents. She's extremely smart with her money and you've never seen her in *The National Enquirer* or on TMZ.

Almost as an afterthought is the fact that, at the ripe old age of seventeen, she has accomplished pop music world domination while diligently keeping up her grades at the local public school and hanging out with life-long friends from back in the day.

Yes, you've seen her at the high-end parties of late. But she's never been anything but polite, considerate and respectful. Her parents have taught her well.

So there you have it. *Lorde: Your Heroine* is a look at how the singer and the person got to be that way. Obviously there is a lot more to come because it would be a downright shame for somebody who has it this together to fall by the wayside.

Forget the cheerleaders and the student body members. You can have your prom queens. If there had been a Lorde back when I was seventeen . . .

. . . I would have been in love.

Marc Shapiro, 2014

DO YOU KNOW HER?

It all seemed to be happening so fast. But then this is pop music in the 2000s, so it shouldn't come as much of a surprise.

Less than a year, three albums (two EPs *True Love Club*, *The Tennis Court* and her debut full length album, *Pure Heroine*) and a handful of smash singles (that included her breakout song "Royals," "The Tennis Court," "Team" and "No Better") removed from obscurity, Ella Maria Lani Yelich O'Connor was about to embark on her first full scale North American tour. She celebrated her seventeenth birthday with the best possible present, a $2.5 million song publishing deal. She had even managed to get a song on the soundtrack of *The Hunger Games: Catching Fire*, one of the biggest movies of the year.

If it were possible for a seventeen year old to sell her soul to the Devil in exchange for immediate success and celebrity, Ella would have to be considered a prime suspect.

No one was more surprised at Ella's overnight success than her father, Victor O'Connor. In a radio interview with *NewsTalk ZB*, he commented, "It's an incredible ride, it's surreal. We always knew she would do well but we never thought that she would do this well."

Her given name is a mouthful. Her stage name is an exercise in attitude, independence with a side of pop feminism and teen angst done up in a whole new, smarter way that has quickly left her teen idol contemporaries in the dust.

This is the worldview according to Lorde.

"I would absolutely take my clothes off if I wanted to," the doe-eyed seventeen-year-old with the exploding mane of curly hair and quietly expressive mouth told *The Telegraph* late in 2013. "That would be my choice and it would be my own choice for empowerment purposes."

Yes, feminism as practiced by Lorde is a big part of the story. Not the whole story by any means, but a substantial enough part that most interviewers can barely go a handful of questions before the F word comes into play.

So bottom line, Lorde is a new breed of feminist, her attitudes are driven by her youth and upbringing. She has not burned her bra. If she has not shaved her armpits it was by choice rather than a symbol of protest. Most of her friends growing up were guys, but she does have a boyfriend and has not held back when she says that all men are not shit.

But she has also proven to be an equal opportunity practitioner of feminist knowledge. She can barely get through an interview without taking aim at other female pop stars she considers an enemy of any feminist movement. In *Metro,* she called Taylor Swift out for being a "flawless, unattainable and somebody who I don't think is breeding anything good in young girls." And she immediately turned a whole faction of teen followers to staring Internet daggers when she made no bones about the fact that Selena Gomez's music was sending the wrong message to young girls.

And when not casting stones at pop stars, she has warmed to the challenge of interpreting a decades old movement for today's women.

"I think that I'm speaking for a lot of girls when I say that the idea of feminism is completely natural and shouldn't be something that's defensive or anti-men," she explained in *Rookie*. "I find a lot of feminist reading quite confusing and that there's often a set of rules and people will be like 'Oh this person isn't a true feminist because they don't embody this one thing.'"

But if you stop here, you're missing the boat because there is more to Lorde beyond whether or not to take off some clothes or to charge into the feminist philosophical battlefield like a modern-day Gloria Steinem.

Unlike many performers who ditch formal education at the first sniff of success, Lorde has made it a personal goal, as well as an acknowledgement to her intellect-first upbringing, to complete her formal secondary school education while balancing it with a rapid rise up the charts.

And while far from being stage parents, Lorde's father and mother are definitely in the picture. Even at this late date, Lorde offered in *New Musical Express* that her mother still makes her lunches and will take her to the studio. The singer conceded in the same article that "I show my parents the stuff I'm doing." And while she does take their opinions into consideration, when it comes to career decisions, her parents know when to step back and leave her alone.

Admittedly there have been some compromises along the way. The recording of her debut album *Pure Heroine* required a three-month vacation from school with the okay from her parents. Otherwise she would make the most of regularly scheduled school holidays. But Lorde has been diligent in hitting the books.

And in case she forgets to do her homework, the young

singer is never far from that "look" from mom. As her notoriety has grown, so has the necessity of Lorde to be away from home. Consequently, when she made her earliest promotional trips to New York, Canada and Australia last year, it was a given that her mother or older sister would be along as chaperone. However, even that bit of business came with an agreement of sorts. Mom could only act as mom. Anything beyond that was strictly forbidden.

Lorde had responded to the question of her comparison to other, paper-thin female pop stars like Taylor Swift, Miley Cyrus and Katy Perry, especially when she made recent headlines when she refused the offer to open Perry's recent world tour. It was a controversial decision, one that, doubtless, cost her a lot of money and exposure. But for Lorde, as explained in an interview with *3rd Degree*, it was a very easy decision to make.

"I turn down a lot of things. I'm a bit picky about what I do and don't do. I think she's (Katie Perry) really talented. I just don't think it was quite right for me. I have a pretty good gut instinct for stuff and if something feels right I'll do it."

It's a difference that she readily compares and contrasts and not always in the most positive terms. Her admirers are not fellow teen stars but rather a more worldly and divergent crowd that has the likes of Kanye West firmly and supportively in her corner.

To her way of thinking it all goes beyond mere comparison but relates totally to her dedication to doing things her way. And it was an indication that while the world was flocking to her in the same way they did to Justin Bieber and other instant pop star flavors of the moment, Lorde was quite adamant in going her own way.

"It's not so much that I just arbitrarily say no to everything," she explained to radio host Ralphie on 95.5 WPLJ. "It's just that I care so much about what I do and I'm concerned about keeping what I do pure."

And one of the first to notice her rugged individuality was Lava Records president Jason Flom. He signed Lorde to his label on the strength of an EP that was literally being given away on the Internet. He explained to *Pollstar* that he was blown away by her music but, perhaps more importantly, he sensed a kind of star quality that does not come along every day.

"Stars to me are, when they walk into a room they take up all the oxygen. She's the opposite of many of today's pop stars. There's something about her that she's not like other people."

She is not fond of doing interviews, and initially avoided them like the plague before she became more accommodating and press savvy. Nor is she a big fan of Facebook and the other offshoots of social media that have been the bread and butter of Bieber and company. It is only with her ascendance in the pop sky that she has reluctantly become more agreeable to doing press. Even with that, she recently told *Billboard*, "If it were up to me there would only be one picture of myself out there."

In a way, she is the modern incarnation of the '30s movie star Greta Garbo, someone who prefers to be in the shadows, a mystery but someone who occasionally pokes her head out to make great music. But with the necessity of fame has come the reality of being a public commodity. She has conceded that to a certain degree but, as she explained in an interview with *The Sydney Morning Herald,* she is making a spirited defense of being just like everybody else.

"Fame is such a weird fucking thing," she asserted. "I try real hard to keep it all a bit real. That's why I insist on taking public transit. I'm not anyone different just because a couple of people have seen my video on YouTube."

Lorde often finds other ways of keeping it real. Like most teens she has what would be called a 'mouth' on her. If something rubs her the wrong way, she will tell you it does and why. And in her first year in the public eye, she has not been shy.

In her blog, *The World According to Lorde*, she acknowledged that Reggae is not her favorite form of music. "I hate Reggae. Reggae makes me feel like I'm late for something." And while she has had a lot of fun in Los Angeles and thinks the fans have been great, she told *The Sun* in no uncertain terms that she could not see herself living there. "I don't think I could ever live in Los Angeles. It does something to your soul. The place really infects people. If I stay there too long, I start being a freak."

At an age when most young pop singers thrust into the limelight would say yes to everything and be literal puppets on the string of calculating management, she has reportedly been quick to say no to anything that rubs her the wrong way. She acknowledged in *Magazine Sunday* that she was using famed Beat renegade writer William Burroughs as her guide to licensing echoing his statement, "Build a good name for yourself because eventually that will become your currency." A pop icon who quotes William Burroughs? I know, it boggles the mind.

A recent article in *Rolling Stone* was full of such forceful 'no's' in which she explained why she refused to do a blatantly commercial video for her single "Royals," and insisted on a leisurely development process that avoided the almost expected quick pop strike in favor of fully developing her creative and performing style. On the wings of her earliest success, she has reportedly turned down massive amounts of money to do things that she felt would present her in conflict with her own personal beliefs and attitudes.

She offered her manifesto in a conversation with *Pop Crush*. "I've turned down easily millions of dollars doing what I do and saying no to things I think are corny. I'm trying to make something people my age will care about. I'm trying to keep my peers feeling like I'm doing something for them and representing them in some way."

Likewise, *Metro* portrayed Lorde as somebody wise beyond her years, smart in the ways of the pop music machine, dealing with people twice her age in an intelligent, logical and direct manner on all elements of her career. Unlike her pop peers, she keeps long hours and gets up early, 7:00 a.m. New Zealand time when there's an interview to do or some merchandising questions to consider. "I'm pretty good at telling people I have to keep normal hours," she explained to *The Observer*. "You can work hard and still make it manageable."

Her Irish/Serbian lineage most likely had something to do with those oh-so-grown-up and, yes, contrary personality traits. It's a mixture known for independent thought and driving ambition. And it is a safe bet that it was those forces that drove her to being something different than your average pop diva.

And make no bones about it, Lorde is definitely a biproduct of the pop music world. Her songs are current with the requirements; a little bit of electro pop, a dollop of teen angst and just the kind of haunting Goth beats and orchestration that make her music fodder for the pop market. Since she proudly proclaims that she does not play an instrument, the emphasis is totally on her vocals and she has done a bang-up job with those; waxing disembodied, often hypnotically matter of fact and darkly contemplative on a plate of lyrics that defies expectations with taut emotions, smart narrative asides and stories that fit quite well in the more safe confines of pop music. But what ultimately differentiates her from the herd is one important thing.

Intellect.

There's a deep, driving, alone-in-her-room confessional quality to what Lorde does. Her much-ballyhooed feminist take is legitimate but ultimately it is less rigid and more even-handed than the feminists of a previous generation. Make no mistake, Lorde's songs are a legitimate and, yes, timely. Just look at the young today. Cliché sentiments and vapid, by the numbers lyrical outs are not part of her creative pallet. Her songs are not without men, love and other coming of age emotions that are universal. Quite simply, she has taken a measured, straight ahead look at the consequences of having them in her life.

With "Royals" being the prime mover in her creative life, much space and explanation has been devoted to dissecting what it and the rest of her songs are ultimately all about. Lorde has given numerous and detailed explanations of her diatribe against those who have and those who have not. But in a recent conversation with *The Sydney Morning Herald*, she ultimately cut to the chase.

"When I wrote 'Royals,' I was telling my friends that I had written songs about our lives. I think a lot of adults thought I was saying something quite profound. But my friends were like 'Yeah we know. What's new?'"

Lorde draws from some widely divergent influences such as classic book authors like Raymond Carver, Tobias Wolff and Sylvia Plath. Her more recognizable musical influences are Prince and Kanye West, and they are balanced out by the 'out there' influences of Grimes, Sleigh Bells, Burial and The Weekend. All these influences drive her toward creating daring music in an often not so daring pop universe.

"I think we're past the whole pop girl thing," she declared to *New Zealand Listener.* "Everything doesn't have to be about the boy. Every song doesn't have to be 'I'm absolutely lost without you.' That whole thing is just tired."

However Lorde is not a one note defiant cry in the wilderness. With the tour of North America only weeks away, Lorde is a constant presence in the nuts and bolts touring meetings. With only a handful of live performances under her belt, she is constantly tweaking and fine- tuning the concert that will showcase her talents to many for the first time.

A bit of a fashion plate, she is diligent in picking just the right clothing to take her act to the stage. She is curious and excited at the idea that merchandise bearing her name and image will soon be available around the world. And, of course, ever vigilant at the prospect of an inferior product going out under her name.

Even with a tour on the horizon and a boatload of music already lighting up the charts, Lorde never seems far from the next thought, the next line scrawled on a scrap of paper, the next impromptu take that sends her voice and her ideas into uncharted territories.

Because unlike many of her peers, Lorde sees herself as an artist with ideas that have so far touched millions. She is a purist, plying her trade in a very commercial universe, with her artistic sensibilities above reproach and not for sale.

This in a nutshell is Lorde. But it is a nutshell that has proven to be as elusive as Mercury.

There is the eccentric, the unpredictable, the seventeen year-old who can occasionally come out to play. After long stints in the studio, she has been known to suddenly just lie down on the floor and be completely uncommunicative. She has also been reported, on several occasions, to suddenly disappear. There's a quietly nervous energy about her . . .

One eye on the quick rocket to the top that has brought her to this point. And one eye on a future that is just around the corner.

CHAPTER ONE

THE CITY BY THE SEA

Devenport, New Zealand is a lot like a lot of places you've passed through on the way to the big city. Places you might have stopped at for a quick bite to eat, some gas and then promptly forgotten.

A seaside suburb just a stone's throw away from Auckland, Devenport is hard on New Zealand's famed North Shore and is known for being the hub of New Zealand's military might as the home of the Devenport Naval Base, as well as for its low key, tourist-oriented main drag which consists of antique shops, bookstores and quaint restaurants.

Years later, Lorde would look back on Davenport, or as it was affectionately known as "The Bubble" in a conversation with *The Guardian*. "It's so insular and closed off from everything," she offered. "It's the kind of suburb that people make movies about."

Lorde has said that growing up in Devenport was an important influence in her songwriting. Lorde addressed the teen angst attached to the city and how it influenced her approach to life. She often recalled that Devenport was, much as it is in many out of the way towns, a kind of a barren life for teens who, typically, had no money, no car and were at an age where boredom and the inability to test the bounds of adulthood put herself and her contemporaries in an emotional shell.

As she grew older, Lorde would often revisit that time when teen angst and the proverbial 'right of passage' usually hinged on not having much to do in the town of Devenport.

"We'd all kick around and everyone would ride bikes everywhere because no one can drive," she told *Spotify*. "There's lots of finding underpasses and tennis courts and places that we would make our own."

She would also make the point on the Swedish television show Skavlan that while they grew up comfortable, she and her peers never seemed to have any money as most teens didn't. "If we wanted to go someplace that was too far to go by bike, we would usually have to take the bus. And then it was, like, 'Okay, we have a dollar but we need another 24 cents, and so then we would be standing around counting out change and hoping we had enough."

But the popular notion that Lorde grew up in poverty wearing rags and struggling to find scraps of food is laughable according to the singer. "I'm not poor," she told *The New Zealand Listener*. "I was extremely lucky. I haven't had times in my life where I've been hungry or anything like that."

But she also admits that as she has gotten out in the world, there has been a growing sense of nostalgia for a life that she has only recently left behind. In a brief but moving video made available through *Vevo Lift* and devoted to grainy black and white scenes from Devenport, Lorde walks through the town, exploring its sights and extolling the simple pleasures of being from there. "I'm happy I grew up there," she intones over the images. "Friday nights. The parties. The beaches. Jumping off the roof of the ferry building. The swimming and the skate-boarding. I'm alright here which is nice."

A big reason for her hometown being her comfort zone has always been a sense of forthrightness and honesty that permeated the town and the people. She has often stated that she learned early in Devonport to take people at their word and to be a quick study when it came to bullshit artists. "I'm glad I grew up there," she said in a *Grammy.com* interview. "I learned how not to be jaded and being from there gave me a chance to figure out who I was."

But the singer, in later years would readily acknowledge that Devenport and nearby Auckland in particular would always be in her head and would go hand in hand with the normal teenage desire to be somewhere else.

"When I was a teenager I ached to get out," she reflected in *Vogue*. "But after I got out and traveled and saw the cities and came back, I was not sure. I had questions. Did I want to grow up? Did I want to leave the suburbs? Where I live is a beautiful place."

Not a lot of people live in Devenport (less than ten thousand at the last census), but those who do have become notorious for being part of a tight-knit community. The local paper, *The Devenport Flagstaff*, was regularly full of stories of the community banding together quite vocally to fight the good fight if something in their community was considered not right.

Devenport is a hardworking middle class town, full of blue and white-collar workers of the 9:00 to 5:00 variety. It was also a welcoming town, which has worn its racial diversity and tolerance as a badge of honor. It's a fairly predictable, simple town that has, surprisingly, had its share of local celebrities. Among those who made headlines over the years are singers Debbie Harwood and Rikki Morris and Olympic gold medal-winner in boardsailing Tom Ashley.

It is in the town of Devenport that Lorde's parents, Vic O' Connor and Sonja Yelich laid down roots. Theirs was a loving and traditional courtship born of equally traditional values and upbringings as well as some liberal leanings that lay just below the surface.

They came into their relationship full of hopes and dreams but with some harsh memories. Both had grown up in strident, closed-in emotional times. It had been that way for their parents and their parents before them. Consequently, Victor and Sonja had very little choice in the matter.

Victor, the youngest of eight children born and raised in Central North Ireland, was the biproduct of a very strict Catholic upbringing. He was raised in a household of no nonsense values and ethics and not a whole lot of warmth. However, he learned much from the former notions and, in years to come, would use them to rise through university, the engineering ranks and finally to become a major player in one of New Zealand's top consulting firms.

Sonja had things equally challenging. Her father, a first generation Serbian immigrant, was a hard worker who never took a day off. Sadly her mother suffered the pains of isolation and was plagued with emotional and mental issues throughout her life. To a large extent, Sonja was left on her own a lot growing up.

She recalled in an extensive article in *Faster/Louder* that, "As a kid, I would often let myself out at night and just walk the streets. I loved the world at night."

That distinct lack of warmth and family softness would follow them into adulthood and, by the time Sonja was pregnant with their first child, a daughter named Jerry, they had promised themselves that any children they had would not suffer the same consequences.

Victor and Sonja had always had designs on a big family and, so, within two years after the birth of their first child (all of their children would be born at home), Sonja was once again pregnant. The months passed quickly as Victor and Sonja, already happily adjusted to the idea of a toddler underfoot, were preparing for their latest addition.

They were not concerned about whether their second was a boy or a girl. Healthy would suffice.

Ella Marie Lani Yelich O'Connor was born on November 7, 1996 . . . Into a world that was everything that her parent's' had not been.

CHAPTER TWO

SPECIAL CHILD

And true to their word, from the moment Ella opened her eyes on the world, she found a family that was warm, welcoming and giving.

Absent from the family atmosphere was the rigidness that had clouded her parents' respective childhoods. Children were not only allowed to be seen and heard in the O'Connor household, but they were readily entitled to an opinion and allowed to experience life on a totally free plane. It would be a child-rearing template that would continue in later years with the birth of Ella's younger sister, India, and younger brother, Angelo.

Ella's earliest memories were of a house filled to overflowing with books and music. It was the rare moment that music was not wafting through the O'Connor household. And as befitting a couple who had grown up in the sixties, the music that was regularly heard was classic.

"My dad's always listened to Neil Young, Fleetwood Mac and lots of soul music like Etta James and Ella Fitzgerald," she recalled to *Spotify*. "As a young kid, I remembered that my parents seemed to have eight to ten albums in constant rotation."

Being the second of what would ultimately be four children was the classic exercise for getting along. Her older sister and she would have the expected spats and arguments over toys and clothes. But there was a more cerebral rather than contentious vibe to their interactions. Problems were usually solved by talking them out.

Bedtime was a special time for the young children. Victor would sing to his youngsters in soft, soothing tones while Sonja, who was slowly coming into her own as a poet of some passion, would read as her daughters sat transfixed.

It was in those earliest years that Lorde, in an NPR interview, would recall how her mother would instill the importance of books in her life. "I think the way that my mum indirectly influenced me is that she always made sure that we were reading in the house and that there were always books around. And we would discuss whatever it was that I was reading."

As she grew older, Ella would recall in *Faster/Louder* that the dinner table would regularly be the center of passionate conversation and family debate on just about any subject. It was during such sit downs that Ella had her first brush with interaction with adults. She instinctively knew when she had something of substance to contribute and those around her would often acknowledge that even as a very young child, she had a knack of taking over a conversation in a mature, for her age, fashion.

"We were super loud and aggressive," she laughingly told an interviewer in a piece for *Faster/Louder*.

However, allowing for the expected childhood acting out, Victor and Sonja's blueprint for child rearing seemed to be working. Even as a newborn and a toddler Ella, as well as her older sister and the two additional siblings to come, were conspicuous by their ease and comfort in this free-flowing family situation that allowed each member, no matter their age, to thrive.

"I come from a big, loud family. My family keeps me grounded. If I don't do something my dad asks, he's like, 'You're not going out tonight.' It's easy to forget that you're not a big deal to anyone you know."

In particular Ella seemed entranced by her mother's reading sessions. How taken she was with the written word would become evident in 1998. In the middle of the night, Sonja was awakened from a sound sleep by a light going on in Ella's room. Sonja shook Victor awake with the fear that somebody had just gone into Ella's room. Victor got up, made his way to Ella's room and opened the door . . .

. . . To find his then eighteen-month-old daughter sitting amid a pile of books at three in the morning, studiously reading.

Victor and Sonja were amazed that a child so young could actually be reading. And although they had always been adverse to any child being tagged with the "gifted" label, they had to admit that there was something quite different and, perhaps, special about their daughter.

And, as they would soon discover, Ella could be quite headstrong as well.

It was not long after the book-reading incident that Ella was dropped off at a mall day care center while her mother did some last-minute Christmas shopping. To occupy the time, the day care supervisors had the children doing a very simple art project. But while the rest of the group followed instructions, the then two-year-old Ella went her own way, dabbing paint on a bit of newspaper. This diversion from the program caught the attention of one of the supervisors who went over to Ella and told her she was doing it wrong.

"I still remember her voice," Lorde recalled years later in a *Rolling Stone* interview. "And I remember looking up at her and being like 'I'm in my own world. I know what I'm doing.'"

That Ella could be so confrontational and defiant with somebody much older than herself had been the much natural byproduct of the youngster being encouraged to interact, not as a precocious child but as a very small equal, with older family members, neighbors and people she would be around in fleeting occasions. Ella was reportedly very convincing when around adults, contributing to conversations in a childlike but adamant and serious way. In such conversations, she would amaze adults in her ability to grasp the nuance, if not the big picture, of an exchange and, yes, contribute.

It was not that the very young child was being deliberately channeled toward older company. She had her siblings and the neighborhood children who she got on well with. But, in later years, she would acknowledge that she always found conversations with those who were older much more stimulating.

Ella turned five in 2001 and commenced her formal education as a student in Vauxhall Primary School. This period coincided with her mother's early steps on the road to becoming an award-winning poet and, not surprisingly, the combination of drive and creativity that had been instilled in Ella from an early age, made the youngster the talk of the school. It was not uncommon in *Vauxhall* for a student to display higher academic instincts even at this early age.

But there was something about the way that Ella approached even the more mundane assignments, a mixture of focus and studiousness, that appeared to her teachers to be above the norm. So much so that, by the end of her first year at Vauxhall, she was the topic of much conversation among the faculty. And all of it seemed to center around the fact that the by now going on six little girl with the curly hair and the secretive smile and demeanor might just be something special.

Years later, Lorde would laughingly dance around the question of how smart and confident she was during an interview on *Skavlan*. "I think I was always kind of faking confidence. Actually I was quite shy. Starting when I was young, I always had this way of plotting, figuring and understanding things. So I guess I was smart that way."

During a meeting with Sonja, one instructor went so far as to state that Ella was truly gifted and that she should be tested. Again that word "gifted." For Sonja it continued to be a word she wanted her child to avoid. But finally she agreed to have Ella take a battery of tests to determine whether or not she was the very word she did not want her daughter to be associated with.

The results of those tests were truly amazing.

The tests indicated that, on many levels, Ella had the mental age of twenty-one. She had high artistic, creative, reading and writing skills and, at the ripe old age of six, she was very much a driven perfectionist. This pronouncement would be the cause of much conversation between Ella's parents.

Victor and Sonja were not so much surprised as dumbfounded. That Ella was showcasing both intellect and drive at such a young age was a true discovery for them. Having those traits could only be a positive. The big question remained as to how to cultivate them?

Against their better judgment, Victor and Sonja enrolled Ella in the prestigious George Parkyn Center for Gifted Education. The school had an excellent reputation as an institution that could help youngsters with seemingly advanced IQs make the most of their talents.

Ella reportedly had no problem adjusting to the new environment. But after only a few weeks, Sonja definitely did and immediately went to the school, picked up her daughter and drove away, reportedly telling Ella, as related in *Faster/Louder* that "You've got to be in this world with everybody else."

Ella went back to Vauxhall Primary and continued to be at the top of her class academically. But Sonja, perhaps still suffering unease from the brush with gifted education, took it upon herself to add to Ella's learning process in her own way. Sonja began to take her daughter out of formal classes on a regular basis to spend creatively nourishing afternoons in art galleries and bookstores and encouraged her to become active in extracurricular outlets as well as her formal subjects.

These were special times for mother and daughter. They would spend time discussing the great artists and authors of the day. That Ella was getting special days off from formal education was part of the allure of being with her mum. That she was absorbing concepts, ideas and notions that interested her was the subtle guide to an intellectually rewarding life.

Ella took the hint . . .

CHAPTER THREE

EDUCATING E

. . . But not without the expected butting of heads between mother and daughter. Sonja made no excuses for steering her young child toward poetry. And Ella had to admit that, as her mother's growing recognition as a published poet of note played out, there was some inclination to like poetry as well. Sonja had a light touch when it came to her daughter cultivating similar literary tastes wanted her daughter to love the poetry form as much as she did. Ella was quick to turn down her mother's poetic advances.

"Mum tried to get me into poetry," Ella recalled in a *The Daily Telegraph* interview. "But I wasn't into it. I did read a lot of short fiction."

But while Sonja lost that battle, she ultimately won the war to mold her young daughter's creative mind. An early edict in the O'Connor household was that there were always books in the house. And as Ella related in *The Daily Telegraph*, the influence of television was ladled out in small doses.

"For a long time, we had a television but no DVD player. Then Mum got a DVD player but only allowed us to watch the old stuff like *Wonder Woman, The Partridge Family* and *Little House on the Prairie*."

Sonja need not have worried about her daughter's mind

being corrupted by the tube. Because shortly after her dalliance with gifted school, she had returned to public primary school with a mind open to any and all opportunities.

When a classmate of hers decided to join the local Devenport Drama Club, Ella went along and was instantly enamored of the opportunity to exercise acting as well as singing talents she had not thought about before. In a conversation with *The Daily Telegraph*, Ella acknowledged the experience of performance as being magic and sacred. "I had to switch on a different side of myself and become a different me."

Drama Club tutor Geoff Allen would acknowledge in a *Faster/Louder* feature that he had a front row seat to just how much of an impact the several years in the club had helped Ella creatively and socially. He beamed as he recalled how Ella learned how to interact with adults and the importance of poise both on stage and in everyday social situations.

Ella proved down to earth on the school ground and made friends easily. But when alone, she would easily revert to a somewhat introverted intellect, always with a book in her hand and, by the time she matriculated to Belmont Intermediate School at age ten, she was, in the best possible way, known around town as the smart girl who was reading grown-up books.

And the names of the authors Ella was reading and, yes, understanding, were quite astonishing, Raymond Carver, Kurt Vonnegut, Sylvia Plath, J.D. Salinger and others. And it was apparent that Ella was not just mentally lifting the heavy tomes for show. At the ripe old age of ten, she was not only reading adult classics but, more importantly, understanding their structure, character and nuance. To her parents and teachers, Ella's reading habits were a source of many conversations. All of them positive.

Years later, Lorde would be quoted in *The Wall Street Journal* paying homage to those and other authors and how they would ultimately influence her once she began to test the songwriting waters. "I began to read a lot of short fiction and I had such a reaction to it. The words were where they should be. I'd read Tobias Wolfe stories out loud to figure out what he was doing to make things rise or crash the way they did."

But having tastes well beyond her years often made Ella the butt of teasing as she made her way through the last days of primary school and into intermediate education. Ella recalled how her esoteric tastes made her the prime target from school-mates less intellectually inclined in an interview with *Rookie*.

"Throughout my intermediate school experience, every-one would tease me for wearing weird clothes, reading weird books and for liking things that other people didn't like. That was hard for me but I developed the attitude of 'I'm above these people.'"

That same year, Ella matriculated to Belmont Interme-diate School, slowly but surely she began, more as a hobby than anything else, writing short stories and developing her own voice. By her own estimation, much of her early literary attempts were either not very good or not memorable.

Lorde chronicled her earliest literary steps in conversa-tion with *Billboard*. "I was eleven or twelve when I was writing short stories. They were probably pretty awful. I wrote a lot of autobiographical stuff and I just wrote total fiction."

And, by way of comparison to what she currently does for a living, Lorde conceded in a *New Zealand Listener* that the idea of writing appealed to her sense of self and solitude. "Before I started to do this, I was really interested in writing short fiction. The reality is that you don't really hear about the stars of short fiction. You're faceless."

Lorde used those early efforts as a mind exercise. They reinforced the fact that she did, indeed, have a fertile imagination and that she could get her thoughts down on paper in a coherent and, hopefully, entertaining manner. But it was anything but serious business.

"Before then I didn't write songs or anything," she related to *The Sydney Morning Herald*. "It was definitely a hobby for me at that point because I had no idea what I wanted to do."

But her 'writing as hobby' approach did not stop her from persisting and, as reported by the local outlets *The Devenport Flagstaff* and *The North Shore Times*, putting her creative writing out in public for the first time.

In 2007 Ella captured top honors in the North Shore Primary School Speech Competition. And a near miss that same year in the Belmont Intermediate School Kid Lit Quiz, that cost the team a trip to Oxford, England for the finals, did not dampen Ella and her classmate's spirit. "We're really glad but we're really annoyed that we couldn't go to Oxford," Ella told the *North Shore Times*. "But we'll be back next year."

The following year Ella and her team placed second in the world in the competition in South Africa. The trip was an eye opener for the young child. Coming from Davenport, travelling to South Africa, seeing its people and another part of the world, Ella absorbed the sights and sounds like a sponge and that trip lit the fuse on the young child's desire to see more of the world.

None of Ella's early accomplishments came as a surprise to the faculty of Belmont Intermediate. From the day she entered the school they had fallen in line with the notion that she was something special.

Ella's former music teacher Jenny Bezuidenhout recalled in a *New Zealand Herald* article that "Ella was extremely talented and that the school gave her a safe environment for her to explore her talents." In the same story another former teacher, Jenny Armitage, said of Ella "She, was an exceptional child who always understood more than other children."

But while exceptional, Ella was still a normal pre teenager who, according to classmate Madeline Christy, who would later play in a school rock band with Ella, told CNN International that "She was always getting in trouble for her uniform because she would always wear bracelets and necklaces."

Christy and Ella were pretty much inseparable during their pre-teen years. They would regularly get together to talk music, go shopping and, she laughingly recalled in an interview with *3News*, spend endless hours trying to figure out what to do with Ella's mound of curly hair. "I remember one time I tried to straighten it and brush it for a disco we were going to and it took me two and a half hours trying to straighten it with her mum helping. It was so funny."

Christy was privy to her friends' hopes and dreams and, when it came to what Ella would do with her life, she recalled that Ella would tell her that she wanted to be a lawyer.

Current acting principal and former teacher Bryan Wynn added to Ella's rebellious reputation when he acknowledged to CNN International that she would always bend the rules by wearing fashionable Doc Martin shoes. Wynn laughingly recalled that he would give her a "gentle reminder' that her shoes were not school shoes and she would always respond with a smile.

As she approached her teen years, many observers felt that the onset of interest in boys and all the normal coming of age challenges would dissuade Ella from her creative and academic pursuits. But if anything, the opposite was true.

Books continued to be her constant companion and her mother would often boast that by the time Ella reached twelve years of age, she had already read a thousand books. Adding to her already growing list of adult literary favorites was the likes of J.D. Salinger, Wells Tower and Junot Diaz. In later years, Lorde would laughingly recall that she would read everything and that the quality of what she was reading was never the criterion.

"I read everything. Good books and bad books. I have to admit that I did read a lot of shit."

But good or bad, books continued to be her go-to place when she contemplated, albeit cautiously, turning her attention to songwriting.

"I've always been a huge reader," she told *The New Zealand Listener*. "I was more into books than I was into music."

But fate and the onset of her twelfth birthday would conspire to change all that.

CHAPTER FOUR

BEHIND HER BACK

Ella was still in the woodshedding stage when it came to her musical attitudes. Like normal pre-teens she had her favorites and was very-attuned to the pop flavors of the moment.

The group Blue was an early favorite. While she would eventually outgrow the pre fab nature of the boy band phase, she told *The Observer* that she found much that was attractive in that kind of pop music and particularly Blue's big hit "One Love." She said of that song, "That song was a gem. I was always drawn to songs with that innate catchiness."

And Ella was nothing if not a true teen expert of the pop music that blared out of the family radio. Ella knew the songs by heart and could rattle off lyrics with ease. She knew where the bands came from, how they got together, and yes, what they had for breakfast. On that level she proved to be a fountain of musical knowledge.

Musically she was also going through an awkward phase where she was listening to bands like Talking Heads, not because she liked the group but because somebody had told her it was a cool group. The irony was that, years later, when her interests had matured she would admit to going back and revisiting groups and finding they had a lot to offer.

However her musical interests went much deeper than the

songs that top 40 radio seemed hell-bent on playing over and over again. She was also drawn to the raw lyricism and emotion of the reigning stars of rap and hip-hop. But her secret pleasure remained the fringe stuff, alternative and progressive pop, the music that only the truly hip and, to her way of thinking, the truly intellectual, could appreciate and understand.

Until she turned twelve, Ella had spent a lot of time alone in her room and in front of mirrors, developing a childish singing style that began with the mimicking of her favorites but was ultimately rounding into shape as something vocally tougher, original and, yes, contrary to the prevailing teen pop world.

Ella's interest in music was well known and she would quite naturally be drawn to friends who had similar interests. They would often sit around talking about the latest pop bands and songs. It was inevitable that at one point, Ella would join a band.

One of Ella's first public performances was as the singer for the rock band Extreme, made up of her schoolmates. Extreme never ventured out beyond school battle of the band's contests at Belmont Intermediate School but, according to *Stereogum*, could always be counted on to present an eclectic mix of covers that would include songs by Richie Blackmore's Rainbow and The Cult.

And even at that stage of musical development, Ella was thorough. When Extreme played the song "Man on a Silver Mountain" at a show, she made sure her audience of other twelve year olds knew it was by Ritchie Blackmore and Ronnie James Dio. When they played "Edie (Ciao Baby)" those kids were educated as to everything Ella knew about The Cult.

As grainy videos of Extreme's performances would indicate, Ella, as lead singer of Extreme, had the early makings of a rock star. Her screaming rock vocals were serviceable, her enthusiasm as she roamed the stage and interacted with the audience was amusing but spot on. Extreme was often dismissed as cute during their short time together. But that Ella had some spark of potential could not be denied.

While at Belmont, Ella had made the acquaintance of classmate Louis McDonald, an only fair guitar player but somebody who shared her budding opportunity to test their musical skills in front of an audience. The pair formed an informal alliance called Louis and Ella and embarked on a brief career as a cover duo playing regularly in what passed for the Devenport music scene.

The pair were regulars at cafes around town and were a big part of the entertainment when the town's Vic Theatre put on shows and were guests on the top-rated Radio New Zealand show, *Afternoons with Jim Mora*. By twelve year old standards, Louis and Ella were considered quite good. Louis was reasonably fit as a guitar player but it was Ella who was primarily responsible for their small-town notoriety.

At that early age, Ella was already projecting a stage presence that was light years beyond her age. Granted, there was not much to her performing style. Basically she just sat and/or stood and sang. But, according to those who saw those very early performances, her singing style was surprisingly mature in an oh-so-controlled and soulful way. Her demeanor was, by contrast, very informal as if she had just popped in to sing and would soon be gone to the rest of her day.

However Louis and Ella were typical twelve year olds of any persuasion and the ongoing conflict seemed to be the difference in their maturity level. Ella was a mature twelve year-old and Louis was not.

On those occasions when they would be approached by even the most softball level local media, Ella was distinct, no-nonsense and to the point in dealing with the press. On the other hand, Louis was your typical twelve-year-old whose responses were often disjointed and stumbling. He made it plain that he was an amateur and that drove the perfectionist in Ella crazy. During their time together, she would regularly admonish him for not being more professional.

Louis and Ella's short stint as local celebrities might have been the end of Ella's musical career. While supportive of their daughter's efforts and talent, Victor and Sonja had a much more academic future in mind for their daughter.

Fortunately Louis's father had other ideas.

Ian McDonald had the makings of the classic stage father. He was well aware that pre- teen and teen performers were being plucked from obscurity and into stardom on a near daily basis and felt his son was talented enough to be the next big thing. His drive to do something about it was encouraged when he read a newspaper interview with Universal Music Group A&R representative in New Zealand Scott Maclachlan that indicated he was always looking for new artists and would gladly listen to submissions.

MacDonald soon saw his opportunity when Louis and Ella were scheduled to appear at their school's talent show entitled *Belmont Idol.* MacDonald videotaped the duo's two song performance of Duffy's "Warwick Avenue" and The Pixie Lott's "Mama Do." For observers of that contest, it was vintage Ella, alternately a world-weary chanteuse and soulful introspective pop belter who, when she did move, presented an image far removed from normal stage performances. It was a safe bet that while Ella was not taking it all too seriously, deep down in her psyche, something was taking a much deeper look. It came as no surprise that Louis and Ella were the hands down winner of *Belmont Idol.*

Ella did not think too much about it. "It was my intermediate school talent show," she offered to MTV. "It was all very low key."

But MacDonald only saw a bright future for his son and was quick to make copies of the performance and send them out to a number of talent agents, with Maclachlan at the top of the list.

In fact he was so intent on spreading the word that he neglected to ask Ella's parent's permission. When Victor and Sonja found out what MacDonald had done, they were understandably irate.

"I was really unhappy about it," Sonja recalled in a conversation with *Faster/Louder*. "I was pissed off. I would never have chosen that for Ella. Not at twelve."

Ella was not as angry as her mother but she was easily more perplexed at being unexpectedly dangled out there for the pop music business to consider. "It was strange to launch myself into the spotlight this way," she told *The Daily Telegraph*. "I had always been the shy, bookish girl."

Maclachlan had his own measure of success before migrating to New Zealand. He prided himself on knowing what the pop business had become and how to channel and mold raw talent into stardom. And one look at the grainy *Belmont Idol* footage told him exactly how he would handle Ella if he decided to take her under his wing.

"The thing that really attracted me to her was her incredible voice," he assessed in a *HitQuarters* interview. He added to his early assessment of Ella's talents when he told *Rolling*

Stone, "Her voice had great depth and timbre. There was real soul to it."

Despite the normal parental reservations, Victor and Sonja made no bones about the fact that they were excited by the unexpected possibilities that could await their daughter in a music career. They knew enough about how the pop music industry worked. A lot of it was 'here today, gone tomorrow' but, in the interim, a lot of money could be made that could set their daughter up quite comfortably as she contemplated her future.

And so when Maclachlan contacted Sonja and suggested they meet at a local café, they readily agreed and met shortly thereafter for an informal sit-down to discuss a possible career for their twelve year-old daughter.

Mother and daughter had no idea what to expect. Maclachlan did have some ideas.

Maclachlan was already mulling over the idea of putting Ella in the studio with a reliable pop music writer to put out some commercial, radio-friendly hits to put Ella on the map. If that did not work, there was always what he considered the standby of doing some covers of '60s chestnuts done up with Ella's soulful vocals. Quite simply, that was the way it had been done and the results spoke for themselves. It worked real well and that's what Maclachlan wanted for Ella.

But his initial impression of Ella as yet another pop puppet on a string was changed once he met her.

Maclachlan immediately "saw her as a perfect storm of a lot of things," he recalled to *3rd Degree.* "Intelligence, charisma, vocals, ability, confidence, humility. She was every box you can tick for an A&R guy."

Those initial impressions of Lorde made it difficult for him to see her being put into a pre fab musical box.

"When I met her, I thought she was just this incredibly intelligent person," he told *HitQuarters*. "It's hard for a twelve year old to know what they really want to do and so we basically just kept up a conversation and I made some suggestions of how we might get some music together."

There had been an immediate meeting of the minds. Ella felt she could trust this much older person and Maclachlan had made a mental note to go with his young charge's every wish. Because he knew in his gut that Ella knew what she wanted and would not back down.

For her part, Ella was immediately at a loss as to how that initial meeting went as she related to *3rd Degree*. "At that time, I really didn't feel that I gave Scott much to go on. I had a voice but I wasn't writing my own songs."

Despite Ella's initial concerns, that first meeting went well and there was discussion of Ella initially being signed to a development deal with Universal Music Group. But before that could happen, Malachlan and she would have to get on the same page musically.

Early on, the A&R man seemed subtly intent on getting his way and offered the youngster a CD of classic '60s music as a gentle prod in his direction. It was at that point that Malachlan found out just how determined Ella was to do this her own way when, shortly after receiving the CD, she tossed it in the dumpster. Ella was not interested in singing cover songs.

"I don't know what he (Maclachlan) was thinking," Lorde related to *3rd Degree*. "But I knew that was not what I was going to be doing. I wanted to do my own thing."

With the arrangement done, Ella would get her first glimpses of what the music business was like. Maclachlan would take Ella around to meetings with representatives of Universal Music Group, the expected meet and greets and introductory get together between the executive branch and their new creative discovery. Ella would relate in a _www.news. com.au_ interview that those she met within those days could be conspicuous by their condescending attitude toward her; as was the case when one record company person called her "a spreadsheet with hair" while well within Ella's earshot.

"People would talk to my manager instead of me," she recalled. "This would usually last for about ten minutes until I would insert the kind of dry sentence that would make most adults splutter and blush and reach for their water. After that, they would start taking me seriously."

Rather than kick this headstrong pre-teen to the curb, Universal Music Group, surprisingly, took her at her word and, at least for the time being, left her alone to do her thing.

"They were pretty open-minded about it," Lorde told _The Guardian_. "They got straight away that I was a bit weird, and that I would not be doing anything I didn't want to do. And so they completely went with that."

But there was a price to be paid.

Ella knew that would mean she would have to begin writing her own songs.

CHAPTER FIVE

DEVELOPMENT HELLO

Maclachlan signed Ella to a development deal with Universal Music Group midway through 2009.

To his way of thinking it was the ideal way to go. Rather than rush her into the studio for a quick strike of songs written by other people or safe commercial covers, Maclachlan instinctively found that Ella was a work in progress and a headstrong one at that.

He could not force Ella, who he acknowledged was wise and mature beyond her years, to do something and have it be successful. And despite her obvious talent, she was still raw and needed some work. A development deal did not require a large expenditure of money and there were no deadlines to meet and so it seemed like the ideal way to go. Which was fine with Ella who had an immediate trust in Maclachlan that he would indeed listen to her as an equal and not a child and, more importantly, that he would do everything possible to have her career go the way she wanted.

The first order of business was to hook Ella up with veteran singing coach Francis Dickinson who would meet with Ella twice a week to work on the tonal quality of her voice and to bring her nasal quality and lower range singing voice up to levels that were pop-music friendly. Ella would recall in *Vogue* that the voice lessons immediately put her in a different frame of mind.

"It wasn't until I had vocal lessons that singing really became kind of a tool and something I could use to get across what I was feeling. Before then the things that I had taught myself to do with my throat were instinctive and stuff that I was mimicking from things that I had heard."

In the meantime, Malachlan was beating the bushes for the best songwriters he could find to work with Ella on crafting her music. He knew this was going to be a difficult process.

Ella had gone into this collaborative songwriting idea grudgingly with her sole caveat being that any songwriter she worked with had to be female. From his perspective, Maclachlan knew that the prospect of established and much older songwriters working with a headstrong singer with zero experience but definite opinions could try everybody's patience.

This period was trial by fire in classic sense, fueled largely by Ella's admitted insecurities with the songwriting process as she explained to *Rookie Magazine*.

"As a young songwriter, I would put a lot of pressure on myself. I'd write a line and then aggressively backspace because I was like 'This isn't a representation of you.' Or 'This is weird.' I would just censor myself so heavily. I felt like there wasn't room for me to write a bad song or write something that didn't necessarily fit in with my vibe or whatever."

Ella's budding musical attitudes were fueled by a growing infatuation with edgier, rather than predictable, pop music. As she would explain to *Red Bull Music*, she was particularly fond of the group Animal Collective. "I was probably twelve or thirteen years old when I really began to discover music. One of the first bands I really liked was Animal Collective. Animal

Collective made pop music but in a way that was new, strange and different."

Lorde would later jokingly recall to *Spotify* that Animal Collective also shot to the top of her hit list for another reason. "I remember thinking 'Dad hates it! This is fantastic!'"

Between 2009 and 2011, Ella would work with no less than a half dozen big names in the songwriting business that had a solid track record for writing hits for other people. The list of those who would attempt to work with Ella included Debbie Swann, Rikki Morris, Karl Steven and Bob Runga. The results of this two-year experiment were abject failure.

If one is to believe the stories from that period, there was little if any chemistry between Ella and these seasoned pros. Reportedly little, if any, writing was being done and no actual songs of any quality were actually completed. And truth be known, the lack of progress was very much in Ella's court.

Ella had it in her head that she was not going to like the experience and that attitude was a classic example of wish fulfillment. In later years, she would complain of that period that she was never feeling like she was completing anything worthwhile and would acknowledge in a *Faster/Louder* piece that, "It was incredibly uncomfortable and stressful."

A major element in the failure of collaboration was the surfacing of her pure artistic instincts that often ran counter to the more commercially oriented attitudes of her collaborators. Lorde admitted as much in conversation with *Red Bull Music*. "I don't just fool around. I'm a control freak. I want my music to sound 100 percent the way I want it to, I try to create art that means something to me."

Maclachlan had a ringside seat for the ongoing writer's block as he offered in an interview with *HitQuarters*. "I put her in with some songwriters and, by trial and error, we went through a few people but it didn't really work. I think she understood that she was going to have to write her own songs."

This two-year drought would have a silver lining. Ella turned thirteen in 2010 and decided it was finally time to try and write her own songs. Not surprisingly, her first efforts were drawn from her everyday life as well as literary and pop culture reference points. A perfect example being the very first song she ever wrote, a dark little ditty called "Dope Ghost."

"My first song was called "Dope Ghost,'" she reported to *MTV*. "I had just watched the Larry Clark movie *Kids* and I thought it was rad. I think it (the song) was poking fun at this girl in my year (class) who was kind of going off the rails."

"It was a diss track," she would relate to *Spotify*. "I wasn't happy that she was letting down our group that way. I also wrote a song about how I had slipped on some rocks in winter and almost drowned. Those early songs were often these strange melodramatic pieces. But then I was only thirteen."

During those early songwriting efforts, Ella was extremely secretive and, perhaps, just a bit embarrassed at her efforts. She grudgingly let her parents in on what she was doing. And that may have been a mistake, as her friend Madeline Christy said to *3News*. "Her mum was the one who told me, 'You've got to listen to her songs.' I wanted to listen to her work for ages and Ella just wouldn't let her (mum) play it. She would just cover the computer. She was really embarrassed about it I guess."

While Maclachlan continued to express frustration at the revolving door nature of songwriters failing to cut it with Ella, he was now faced with a whole new set of challenges now that Ella was striking out on her own.

Maclachlan recalled in *HitQuarters* that it was a nurturing process centered around Ella finding herself as a songwriter. He was encouraged by the fact that the youngster's earliest songwriting efforts, (yes even "Dope Ghost") had shown some promise.

"It was really all about feedback and making practical suggestions about arrangements, melodies and stuff like that," he related.

The explanation sounded simple enough but, as it would play out in the ensuing months, it was a lot of back and forth between the two. Ella would bring Maclachlan something she had been working on and he would make comments that she would take into consideration or completely discount. Then she would go away and, sometimes as many as three months later, she would come back with something else that, to her mentor's delight, always seemed to be an improvement.

Going into late 2011, Ella was still in a state of slow but steady development. Her songwriting skills were getting sharper but Maclachlan was still adamant that she needed an experienced guiding hand to add some elements of musical and production direction to her raw but promising talents.

By this time, Ella had matriculated to Takapuna Grammar and had fallen in with a much hipper crowd who, upon hearing about Ella's entry into the pop music scene, were very supportive and, yes, occasionally teasing. Ella had the cool factor on her side at this point but it was, in the eyes of her tight circle of friends, only a facet of her personality, and they were quick to treat her just like a regular person.

It also helped the socialization process that Ella's parents insisted that she continue to attend public school and that, while she would sometimes miss days because of her music career, she would never fall behind in class and continue to shine at the head of her class.

When it came to her home life, Ella's parents made sure she was grounded. The chores she had before she suddenly became a budding pop star were still there and she was expected to do them. And that did not stop at doing the dishes and taking out the garbage. When Sonja was putting the finishing touches on her long-in-the-works Master's thesis, she turned to her daughter to do the final edit. Long story short, Ella made short, accurate work of her mother's 40,000 word thesis. Sonja got an A.

It went without saying that Ella's critical eye when it came to things like school essays and term papers also made the rounds of her classmates who would regularly enlist her to go over their work. That would ultimately backfire when they would complain that what they had done was not perfect and could be better. "I became very particular," she told *The Wall Street Journal.*

The last few months of 2011 were a blur. The constant challenges of trying to get a foothold in the music business had, to a large extent, turned into an actual job, resplendent in failed writing attempts and collaborations that were seemingly going nowhere. But Ella maintained a stalwart stance, conceding that the pop music scene, flavors of the moment to the contrary, could take some time, especially when, by design, she seemed a lot more driven and different then the hit makers of the day.

November marked her fifteenth birthday and it passed with little, if any, highpoints other than, chronologically she had become a girl of a certain age. She was happy to be with family and friends and seemed satisfied with that gift. What

Ella did not know was that a more tangible gift was just around the corner.

The word along the music industry grapevine at this point was that Ella was only one hit single away from being a superstar. Consequently Maclachlan was constantly being bombarded by agents and managers looking for a chance to get one of their songwriting clients in the door. One of the more persistent had been Ashley Page.

Page had heard Ella sing and so felt she had the ideal person to collaborate with. It had been a soft sell that had been off and on for two years. Finally, with seemingly no other songwriter on the horizon, Maclachlan agreed . . .

To meet Joel Little.

CHAPTER SIX

MAGIC

Even before she met Joel for the first time, Ella knew all about him.

Joel was a member of the New Zealand based pop punk band Goodnight Nurse that had spent years on the high school and local club and concert circuit throughout New Zealand. Goodnight Nurse sold some albums, had a couple of minor hits but were one of those bands that, after nearly a decade, could not break out of New Zealand and disbanded.

She was less aware of his musical change of life. What she discovered was that Joel had gone through a very real midlife crisis of sorts. He had given up the endless road to seemingly nowhere and the sporadic but ultimately unfulfilling success to learn about the production side of music and more modern sounds. Through hard work he had risen to some semblance of notoriety in the industry as the guiding light to such notable performers as Dane Rumble and The Peasants.

Maclachlan met with Joel and came away quite impressed as he explained in *HitQuarters*. "He's a very laidback and generous producer. He doesn't have a big ego and he did not come across as someone who would patronize Ella."

Ella and Joel met for the first time in December 2011. That he had never heard her sing only added to the awkwardness of that first meeting as he recalled in an interview with *The New Zealand Herald*.

"I just remember her coming in (to the studio) and us both probably feeling a bit odd," he said. "It's quite a weird situation when you sit down with someone you've never met before and try to write a song."

But he recalled in a *3rd Degree* conversation that any doubts he had were erased the first time he heard the young girl sing. It immediately became clear to Joel that she was a natural and that it was meant to be. "I heard her voice and I was like 'This is a ridiculously good voice.'"

The first few times they met it was a feeling out process, discussing at length the type of music they liked, what kind of sound she liked as well as things that had nothing to do with music. And what they discovered was that their musical tastes, as it pertained to the edgier forms of pop, were similar and, perhaps most importantly, that there was an instant connection in terms of personality.

Joel was quickly made aware of the baggage that Ella had brought to the table. Her two years of attempting to write with other songwriters had not been pleasant and had, potentially, made dealing with Joel an even bigger challenge. But what he soon found out was that her previous experience had some positive points. "I remember early on she was like 'I just want to write with people to figure out if I even want to do music,'" reported the New Zealand Musician.

Ella sensed that Joel was going to be a good match. "Joel is a lovely person," she would recall in conversation with *3rd Degree*. "He was the type of person who could take what was already there and make it better."

"We started working on trying to figure out what she

wanted to do, just playing with different sounds and different styles," Joel told *The New Zealand Herald*. "There was never any pressure to be anything in particular. It was just write some songs and see what happens."

What happened, initially, was not much.

Into 2012 and in the early stages of their collaboration, both were still attempting to feel each other out creatively. Joel admitted that when Ella brought in her lyrics, he had a hard time getting over his feeling that they might not work within the context of a song. He would change his mind when he heard the young girl sing them. Their first series of sessions would end in February when, true to her word, Ella had to put aside music and return to school. And, according to Joel, it did not end too well.

"Our first few songs together were so shit," he told *Louder/ Faster*.

It was not the most encouraging way to end their first round of work as Ella returned to school. Now in the equivalent of American high school and temporarily removed from the pressures of a career that was seemingly going nowhere, the pressure was off to a degree. Ella was around old friends where she basked in the glow of being a bit of a schoolyard celebrity. She would often state that her friends at that point were "chill" when it came to her growing celebrity and would only occasionally jokingly snap pictures of her with their cell phones.

For her part, Ella was more than willing to play at being the local celebrity by putting on occasional impromptu concerts for her classmates. Principal Simon Lamb recalled those moments when he told *The New Zealand Herald,* "She has an amazing voice, a lovely voice."

On most nights she would be at home, doing the dishes

and other odd chores. The prospect of stardom had not affected her. She was happy to be the normal kid at home, content and comfortable around her family. Ella also continued to excel academically and was being actively considered for the advanced International Baccalaureate Program, a sure step to any university of her choosing if she saw higher education in her future.

However she was not neglecting her musical pursuits. She was constantly at work on songs and, to her own way of thinking, found that she was getting better at it. She could not wait until the April school holidays when she and Joel could meet up again.

Since they began working together, Joel and Lorde were never seemingly too far from the gentle hovering of her parents. Calls from home were sporadic, the simple parental concerns of how it was going and had she eaten. Sometimes Lorde would head those calls off at the pass by texting or calling on her own to make sure her parents knew what was going on and how the sessions were going.

But occasionally the pair would get so caught up in making music that they quite literally lost all track of time. And, as Joel related in *3rd Degree*, he would occasionally have to deal with the wrath of Sonja. "We've had times when it's been midnight and I've just really forgotten to say 'Do you need to call your parents or anything like that?' Then I'll get a text from her mum, saying 'Where the hell is my daughter?' And I'm like 'Oh shit, that's right.'"

Sure enough, Joel noticed an immediate maturity and catchiness in Ella's songs, the best of the bunch being "Million Dollar Bills," a musical moveable feast chronicling the age old battle of emotion, independence and what would be Ella's favorite targets, conspicuous consumption. And like all of her songs, the lyrics reflected her reality.

"I'm not thinking when I'm writing," she explained to *New Zealand Listener*. "But with my lyrics, everything is personal. Everything has happened to me and all the things tend to build up this kind of fabric that people can, hopefully, relate to."

Joel immediately set to creating the musical backbone for "Million Dollar Bills," adding just the right amount of fringe elements to the pop gloss and making the center piece a clever technology-driven sampling of Ella's voice. For Joel, working with Ella became a crash course in doing things differently.

"I basically had to re-adjust my approach to make the music suit what she was saying to capture, through the music and the melody, the essence of what the lyric was," he explained to *New Zealand Musician*.

Ella spent the next few months in school but found herself easily distracted by the progress that was being made with Joel. It seemed that every waking moment was spent at her laptop, writing and refining lyrics and song structure. Joel had already blocked out four days of studio time in July to work with Ella who was sensing a turning point in the odyssey to getting her songs out into the world. And so she wanted to provide him we the best she could create.

Two songs, "Bravado" and "Biting Down," turned out to be very emotional creations. Lyrically they were spot on, the imagery was ripe with observational and confessional opportunities. And Ella was rounding into shape in terms of thinking with both her already potent voice as well as the musical backbone that Joel would most certainly contribute.

Finally there was a song that Ella was feeling emotionally attached to on a number of levels.

... "Royals" ...

Originally the idea of "Royals" had been as more of a minor song, a semi-mocking look at the modern aristocracy and their conspicuous wealth. A few preliminary lines had seemed promising but what finally kicked the notion of "Royals" was a chance look through an issue of *National Geographic.*

"I had this image from *National Geographic* of this dude just signing baseballs (actually a member of the Kansas City Royals major league baseball team), she recalled in an interview with VH-1. "He was a baseball player and his shirt said 'Royals'. I was taken by the image and that word. It was all just really cool."

That the lyrics to "Royals" also take dead aim at the modern aristocracy of celebrity and pop culture figures also figured into Ella's influence for the song and was part and parcel of her long held interest in history and historical figures. "Obviously I've had a fascination with aristocracy my whole life," she added in her VH-1 conversation. "Like the kings and queens of 500 years ago, they were like the rock stars of today."

Ella's infatuation with hip hop and rap music was also playing a part in the way she wrote the lyrics. What had been an afterthought was now evolving into a major songwriting effort with far-reaching potential.

When Ella and Joel got together again in July, her collaborator was happily amazed at the songs Ella had brought in. They immediately set to work creating melodies and beats to fill out the songs. It was a magical, mystical week for the pair. Quick trips to a nearby restaurant were only out of necessity, after which they would literally race back to the studio. By the end of the week "Royals",, "Biting Down" and "Bravado" were, for all intents and purposes, in their completed form.

And while experience had taught him to be cautious, Joel acknowledged to *3rd Degree* that he got a good buzz off "Royals." "When we finished up and I listened back for the first time, I sensed there was something about this song. I wasn't thinking that it would go as crazy as it did but I knew that there was something magical about this track."

But ultimately it would be Maclachlan whose opinion would matter the most. He came in at the end of the week and, after some small talk, sat silently as Ella and Joel played him "Bravado" and "Royals." Ella recalled to *Faster/Louder* what happened next.

"Scott came in and listened. I remember him swearing a lot. He was pretty happy."

The consensus was that they had done good work. With Ella's haunting vocals and different take on the pop music landscape and Joel's pristine, often haunting and ultramodern production, there was a definite "cool" factor in what they had created. But nobody saw a worldwide hit in those early songs.

The reason being that while they were, to a song, outstanding, Maclachlan sensed that they were just too different to conform to what the music business considered hit worthy. Of course, this was something he kept to himself.

It was in this moment of total euphoria that it was determined that while Ella was nice, she would need a dynamic stage name to put her musical persona over the top. Ella had not been real keen on the idea of branding and a lot of the ins and outs of the pop music business. But she had readily agreed to the stage name idea, looking to her literary and historical interests for inspiration and eventually finding something that seemed to work.

Ella had always been a royalty buff from a very young age. She was completely fascinated by those who had been born to rule and what the concept of what true royalty was all about. She knew a lot about royalty. Now it seemed she was about to become royalty.

"When I was trying to come up with a stage name, I thought Lord was really rad but very masculine," she said to *Vulture* and endless other outlets. "Ever since I was a little kid, I have really been into royals and aristocracy so to make Lord really feminine I just put an E on the end."

And so Lorde was born.

CHAPTER SEVEN

I'LL SHOW YOU

Encouraged by those early studio successes, Joel and the now newly christened Lorde continued to churn out solid songs at a steady pace. Before they knew it "Bravado," "Royals," "Million Dollar Bills" and "Biting Down" were joined by a reworked version of The Replacements' "Swingin' Party" and "The Love Club," as well as a handful of other songs and remixes waiting in the wings.

Given the success they had in Joel's studio creating the music, it seemed almost a given that the completed songs would be recorded, in a very sparse instrumental setting, in the same studio.

"It took three weeks," Joel related in *New Zealand Musician.* "Most of the songs came together in a couple of days. But we were doing proper studio twelve-hour days which is a lot for somebody not used to that. But she took to it."

The chemistry Joel and Lorde had established was mirrored in the recording sessions. As the de facto producer, Joel continued the patient, encouraging influence. When things needed a slight tweak or he felt another take was necessary, he knew exactly how to broach it to Lorde. For her part, Lorde's trust in Joel was now complete. There were those moments when the pair agreed to disagree and, in those cases, the young singer usually got her way. But the feeling at the end of the sessions was that they had enough really solid material for a first rate introductory EP.

And that "Royals" seemed the perfect, albeit unorthodox, first single.

Maclachlan took "Royals" to the Universal Music Group promotion department for their opinion. He would not like what they told him.

"They said that radio would never play the song," recalled the exasperated Maclachlan in a *Rolling Stone* feature. "And if you don't have radio support, you're fucked. So we either had to go on bended knees and try to convince them or, fuck it, we had to put it out for free."

That Maclachlan was so quick to toss aside his staunch by-the-books music business attitude and even consider such a risky move was surprising. He had not been with Universal Music Group that long and was not inclined to ruffle any corporate feathers. And to give something away for nothing, despite the minimal investment of corporate money to that point, would definitely rub the bean counters the wrong way. But it appeared that a bit of Lorde's determination had rubbed off on him and Maclachlan was all in.

And, as he recalled in *HitQuarters,* money be damned. "We felt it was a very strong piece of music and thought 'let's just put it out now and worry about the money later.'"

As it turned out Lorde/Ella already had a pretty good working knowledge of the Internet. "I have always been inter-nationally-minded with how I consumed music and art," she explained to *Billboard.* "Everyone has the internet now, so it doesn't feel like as much of an impediment. I grew up listening to people who made music in their bedrooms and put it up on SoundCloud. So I kind of thought that the opportunities were limitless."

Lorde quickly created a Facebook, a Twitter, a Tumblr and a SoundCloud account and went live with all the accounts on her own Facebook profile. Then Lorde could do nothing except sit back, wait and hope.

The singer would look back on this decision to give her music away sometime later in an interview with *Spin*.

"It was one of those choices where the record company was saying, 'Uh, okay, you shouldn't do this.' But I felt really strongly about it. I was fifteen years old when I put that music out. I didn't want it to be about how much money I could make off it. I just wanted people to hear it and to like it. It felt right for me."

Lorde would often acknowledge that she had low expectations for this giveaway and assumed it would wind up being a freebee for her friends and nothing more.

For his part, Maclachlan was working behind the scenes to keep an air of mystery behind the release. No photo or bio of Lorde was made available and there was never any mention of the singer's age. He was determined to let the music speak for itself.

The response to her free musical offering was not long in coming. Within a few hours of its posting, Lorde discovered that 300 people had decided to give *The Love Club* a listen. She reasoned that since she did not have 300 friends, she might be onto something. Something was not long in coming as the number of downloads rose to 10,000 in the first few days.

"I wasn't expecting *The Love Club* EP to do what it was doing, not by a long shot," she related in *Sunday Magazine*.

"I tweeted Joel about it and I used the word 'booyha,' Look at us now."

The approach to getting Lorde out there worked. Within six weeks, Maclachlan had reportedly received calls from just about every record company in America. But it went without saying that with his long-standing development deal with Universal Music Group in place, he was not going to jump ship.

While the initial response to her music was a surprise to everyone concerned, it was still quite early in the game to declare that a star was suddenly born. However Lorde would recall in *The Observer* that there seemed to be an inevitability about what was suddenly happening around her.

"I wasn't necessarily saying that I would be famous. But there were requests from labels and people were pulling overseas. There was a sense of a huge change approaching."

The giveaway continued to roll. Within a few weeks, the free music had resulted in more than 60,000 downloads. Universal Music Group realized their mistake and called a halt to the giveaway.

But not before *The Love Club* had come to the attention of the Universal Music Group American subsidiary label, Lava Records. The company president, Jason Flom wasted little time in getting on the horn with Maclachlan. A deal was struck. Quite simply it had been Flom being first to call, as well as his reputation for coveting and breaking new, edgier performers, that had sealed the deal.

The next few months were a whirlwind of quiet but persistent activity.

Lorde and Joel were in the studio at every opportunity and quality songs continued to flow from the collaboration. Maclachlan, who for all intents and purposes had become

Lorde's de facto manager, took it upon himself to contact and eventually sign a deal with US concert promoters Windish Agency, a lesser known agency but albeit one that had a reputation for positive results with more artsy, fringe performers. such as Foster the People and Goyte. This was considered a bold move as it would be another six months before Ella stepped on a performing stage for the first time as Lorde.

Tom Windish had built a reputation as a progressive rebel in the touring industry. An instinctive eye and ear on talent off the beaten path, he could reportedly size up talent very quickly. As he explained in a *Chicago Sun Times* interview, he formed an opinion on Lorde almost immediately.

"The quality of her songs were undeniable," he said. "The lyrics, the beats, the melody, the story. I could tell she was authentic."

Neil Harris, manager of two of the Windish Agency artists Cut Copy and Dragonette, and who also related that he was in synch with the way Maclachlan wanted Lorde to be present to the world stage, said, "I knew Scott wanted her to be presented as a left field artist who wasn't shoved down everyone's throat. Windish is probably better at that than anybody. They've got cool for lack of a better word."

Lorde turned sixteen amid this rush of activity, normally a milestone in a young girl's life. The prom would be coming up soon and the always fashion-conscious Ella had to have the perfect dress. There were also term finals to consider and the seemingly never-ending pile of dishes that needed to be washed.

Turning sixteen was made more important by the fact that her talent and the fates had brought her to the brink of stardom at such a young age. There was a constant air of anticipation and excitement as Ella temporarily put aside the Lorde persona in favor of some relatively normal family and school time. But as she began, often grudgingly, to do more promotion and her story began to unfold in a public arena, it became evident that Lorde was beginning to become the dominant force.

Things tend to move a bit slower once a major label takes over and, while Lava Records was inclined to move at light speed, Universal Music Group was taking a traditionally more leisurely approach to unleashing *The Love Club* on the world. Early reports indicated an official digital release in the first quarter of 2013 and a CD release to follow two months later.

But behind the scenes, Lava Records' head Jason Flom had other ideas.

CHAPTER EIGHT

"ROYALS" FLUSH

Flom knew technology. He knew youth culture, which lived and died by the Internet, texting and tweeting. He knew that would be the way to break Lorde very big and very fast.

And with the official digital download of *The Love Club* now set for March 2013, Flom knew that he had to move fast. Which meant getting a copy of *The Love Club* to Sean Parker.

Parker, Napster co-founder, former Facebook president and an early *Spotify* backer and head of one of *Spotify's* most influential music platforms, *Hipster International,* had a golden ear when it came to identifying superstar talent in the making. Parker respected Flom's instincts enough to immediately give Lorde a listen. He liked what he heard as he explained to *Forbes.*

"I feel like, in many ways, she's the antidote to disposable pop music," he said. "There's obviously something more authentic and personal in Lorde's music. I get the sense that she represents the return to a singer/songwriter approach to songwriting."

And as Parker would prove, he was all action when it came to getting "Royals" off to a flying start.

The first shot was fired on March 19 when the track "Royals" was added to the *Spotify* platform. Locally Lorde not surprisingly burst out of the gate as well. "Royals" debuted at No. 1 on the *New Zealand Top 40* charts and would remain at that position for three weeks. On that same day *The Love Club* EP debuted at No.2, beaten out for the top spot by the latest release by David Bowie.

With the growing notoriety, the people on the management side felt it was time to drop the cloak of mystery surrounding what Lorde looked like (to that point there had only been one photo) and to finally reveal herself. Lorde's first full-blown photo shoot would take place that month in conjunction with an appearance in the *New Zealand Listener.*

Reportedly Lorde was comfortable in front of the camera lens and at ease with the photographer directing her in different poses that, largely, played to the notion of her as a Goth/Pop intellect. The singer was now officially out there for the whole world to see.

Then, as part of an early ramp up to the May 2013 release of *The Love Club* CD, "Royals" was added to the coveted *Hipster International* site on April 2. "The moment Lorde's "Royals" was added to Hipster International's playlist, we saw an immediate reaction from around the world," Flom told *Forbes.*

Six days later "Royals" made its entry on the *Spotify Viral Charts.* Lorde took an active role in that early promotional push, shooting interview and performing footage that was turned into what was called a *Homepage Takeover* to promote the single. By early May, "Royals" had reached No. 1 on the *Spotify Viral Chart.*

The immediate success of "Royals" had Lorde in a bit of a tizzy emotionally. The song was important to her in so many ways. But now that it was literally everywhere on the Internet, she was a bit perplexed as she offered to *New York Magazine.*

"I experienced such a disconnect with that song. Everyone knows its bullshit. But somebody had to write about it."

For a song so spot on and pointed in its lyrical dissection, it was inevitable that "Royals" would have its controversy and at least one very vocal detractor. In a column for the website *Feministing*, writer Veronica Beyetti Flores took "Royals" to task for what she considered its racist attitude, citing the use of such words as 'gold teeth,' 'Cristal' and 'Maybach' as evidence of anti-black sentiments. She said, "Why shit on black folks and rappers?"

The charges against "Royals" and, by association, Lorde generated just enough traction that the singer, in a *Rookie* interview felt obligated to address them. "When highly respected writers start to question what you're doing, you start to question what you're doing and, if you've done something wrong, you think about it. But I do think people were using those words to make their arguments. I was not using those words to target rappers and black people. Those kinds of things are about the excess of pop culture in general and not about any specific group."

Lorde's explanation seemed to mollify her critics and the racist charges quickly disappeared.

With the CD version of *The Love Club* due to be released in a matter of days, Lorde had to begin to deal with the sudden clamor to see her perform live. But after due consideration, the singer and Maclachlan decided on brief sets at small out-of-the-way clubs to get her feet wet. Which meant that Lorde was suddenly in need of some musicians.

Maclachlan went through his Rolodex and discovered that keyboard player Jimmy MacDonald and drummer Ben Barter seemed to fit the bill. Both were veterans of a number of different musical genres, had extensive touring credentials, were respected session musicians and were very laidback. More important on a personal front, they did not have any problems backing and taking orders from somebody half their age. Ultimately, and even more important, they had the requisite technological chops to make Lorde's admittedly minimalist sound much bigger and resounding in a live setting. Lorde would be the final decision. MacDonald and Barter, who were in the United States when they received the call, immediately flew back to New Zealand and, after some conversations and informal rehearsals, Lorde gave the pair a thumbs-up for the gig.

The sites chosen for Lorde's first live shows were the Mighty Mighty Club in Wellington and Gatalos in Auckland. Both clubs had a reputation for looking kindly on new acts and their intimate nature made an ideal first step for Lorde. Allowing that Lorde, despite her outward composure, would be nervous at her first live dates, Maclachlan made a point of not inviting the media. But word spread quickly, in particular when it came to the very tiny Mighty Mighty Club.

On the night of her performance at the Mighty Mighty Club, Lorde was a bundle of nerves as she, two roadies and her musicians arrived for their soundcheck. Lorde, despite her best efforts, was an emotional trainwreck.

"I was nervous," she told *3rd Degree*. "It was bad. I was very stressed out. There was a lot emotionally invested in me as an artist and I was thinking that I've got to deliver."

The first song she played that night was 'Bravado'. A bold first statement on a very shaky night.

As reported in *Stuff*, the first show, with a capacity of 140 seats, sold out in 73 seconds. A second show was not far behind, with those who could not get in clamoring for a third show to be added. Lorde remembered the night in an interview with *New York Magazine.*

"I played my first show in May. I was so nervous. It was real small, about 120 people or something like that. The room was filled with my friends. It was such a strange feeling. I had never been in a situation where everyone was there to see me."

By all accounts those first performances were a success. The songs carried additional substance and emotion in a live setting. Despite the nerves, Lorde seemed ultimately at ease in the spotlight and reportedly warmed to the situation and, by show's end, was at ease in front of the appreciative audiences.

The one thing audiences of those early shows noticed was that Lorde did not move like most pop stars. There was a kind of spasmodic sense of time and space in her moves in which a mixture of mindless and impressionistic guided her steps. The singer knew that it was different when she talked to *The Wall Street Journal.* "I'm too weird as a performer to copy anyone else," she explained. "I kind of thrash around. I know it's unsettling to look at. But the truth is that I can't dance."

Nobody was more relieved than MacDonald and Barter who had taken a big chance by relocating back to New Zealand on a wing and a prayer for a couple of very small club dates. But as the drummer offered to *3News*, they had done an equally solid job on very short notice. "At the start, we didn't know if we were doing a good job or not. When we first came from the States, we expected session musicians to step in at some point and be like 'Okay, we'll take it from here. Just go home!'"

MacDonald was even more succinct in conversation with *New Zealand Musician.* "I don't know what I expected. All I wanted was to be on tour. If I could have enough money to survive and be on tour, that's all I wanted."

Fortunately the powers that be in the Lorde camp were dually impressed and the pair were immediately offered permanent positions in the band.

The Love Club made its long anticipated CD release in May. The hype machine at Universal Music Group had been working overtime. Now it was time for the critics to have their say. And they would.

Allmusic praised the lyrical content of the release, describing it as "electro pop meditations on life, love and the eternal joys and pains of youth." *The New Zealand Herald* chimed in, praising Lorde's voice saying, "it seems to come from someone twice her age." *The Nelson Mail* also focused on the strength of Lorde's vocals, describing her voice as "impressive and smoky"..

Typical of Lorde, she was excited yet subdued at the impact *The Love Club* was having on her. The singer admitted to *New York Magazine* that she was also getting her fair share of the downside of sudden celebrity.

"Now I get recognized, which is weird. People come up to me when I'm in a restaurant and I've got a mouthful of food. I've also had to change my Facebook account because I've started getting messages from dudes saying we're going to be the best of friends."

Prior to the release of "Royals," it had been a foregone conclusion that Lorde would make an accompanying video. Lorde had not been averse to making a video but, as she explained to *The Huffington Post*, it had to be done on her terms. Which would mean that, with a couple of brief exceptions, Lorde would not appear in the video.

"The music video for me was all about creating a piece of

art," she said of the video which was directed by Joel Kefali. "I wanted it to be cinematic and to be something you can immerse yourself in."

To that end, the "Royals'" video was very much a do-it-yourself effort. Shot in and around her hometown, it offers up segments featuring her friends from school doing seemingly mundane things as the music weaves in and out of the scenario.

"The song and the video were my attempt to keep it real," she said in a *Bullett* interview. "Basically I got a bunch of my friends to jerk around and do nothing for a day and we filmed it. I guess what I was trying to do was to let other people my age know I was feeling the same as them."

The "Royals" video made its debut on May 12 and had gathered more than 100,000 hits within the first 24 hours.

Nobody would blame Lorde if she had taken a bit of a break. "Royals" and *The Love Club* were just beginning to take off in the rest of the world, including the all-important US charts and had insured this first round of songs a long run.

But Lorde did not work that way.

CHAPTER NINE

TENNIS ANYONE?

After the immediate and resounding success of "Royals" and *The Love Club* EP, the expectations were that a full-length album would next be in the offing. The last thing anybody expected was another EP containing three previously released songs and one new song, the projected new single "Tennis Court."

But the prevailing attitude between Lorde and her backers was a need to prime the pump one more time before a full album was released. Thus the single "Tennis Court," a song that reflected Lorde's abiding interest in looking back as well as confronting her current status in the often alien territory of the music business.

Lorde had never played tennis but, as she explained to VH-1, she had always looked upon a tennis court as "as a symbol of nostalgia and beauty." As for the song's slightly jaundiced look at her present state in the music business, she explained to *Macleans'* that it was a detached look at the nature of the beast.

"I wrote my song 'Tennis Court' after having had a glimpse into the music industry and I was thinking how superficial people can be and how we put up all these fronts."

In hindsight, "Tennis Court" may well have been a more

pointed and attacking song than "Royals." Its jagged obser-
vations appeared more tough and universal in tone and not
quite age specific as "Royals" had been. It was hard to argue
that "Royals" was easily one of the best songs of the year but a
strong case could be made for "Tennis Court" as a more relat-
able one.

By this time the chemistry between Lorde and Joel had
become so instinctive and ingrained that they would often go
hours without speaking in the studio, each attending to their
own elements of her music before meeting in the figurative
middle to exchange ideas. But as Joel related in an interview
with *Billboard*, the occasion of "Tennis Court" would add a
new twist to their creative relationship.

"Up until that point she would always bring lyrics and we
would take inspiration from those as to where to go with the
music. But with 'Tennis Court,' this was one instance where I
started putting the music together and she would be writing
the melodies. That song was one where we had everything but
the chorus. She was sitting in the back of the room while I was
working on the music and she said, 'I think I've got a chorus
idea.' I said, 'Let's hear it,' but she said 'no. It wasn't ready yet.
Once she had it, she basically sang the entire chorus and I was
like 'Holy shit! This is seriously good.'"

The completed song was a droning industrial mix of pop
and art rock that meshed perfectly with Lorde's trademark
disembodied/disinterested vocal shadings. A song this dark
and brooding was tailor made for an accompanying video and
Lorde was happy to oblige; once again enlisting the services of
director Joel Kefali to film a truly surreal, haunting video. In
it, Lorde is pictured in a tight close-up wearing black clothing
and lipstick with her hair braided. As "Tennis Court" plays

in the background, the singer stares silently into the camera. She does not lip sync, except for the word "yeah," which she mouths several times as she fades in and out of blackness. Lorde's reputation as an artsy minimalist champion when it came to videos was further enhanced by "Tennis Court."

The single "Tennis Court" debuted digitally on June 7, 2013, the same day as the *Tennis Court* EP was made available. Critics who had only a couple of months previously been tossing about the good word on "Royals" were rushing out new superlatives in praise of her second single.

New Musical Express praised the song for its "forward looking genres and Lorde's strong pop vocals". *Grantland* called the song "a murkily winsome ever so slightly chopped balled." And even superstar Elton John could not resist commenting on the song to *USA Today* when he said 'Tennis Court' was "one of the most lovely beautiful things on earth."

"Tennis Court'" would debut at No. 1 on the *New Zealand Singles Charts* and would become the second cog in the Lorde chart explosion to make June 'The Month of Lorde.'

On June 10, the already well-entrenched "Royals" cracked the US market on the *Billboard Alternative Rock Radio Spins Chart*. The song continued its monster status on *Spotify*, cracking the Top 100 List. Into July, Lorde's music continued to make chart noise, debuting on the *Billboard* Hot 100 List.

With only less than ten songs to her credit, Lorde's immediate, worldwide success was evident. In a short period of time, her songs had charted on no less than fifteen foreign charts. Even the non-singles were getting play. It remained for only one country to bow down to Lorde.

Despite the instant success Lorde had in Europe, America was considered the final frontier for any budding pop star looking to break into the big time. And so Lorde had seemingly arrived early in July when the *Australian* and countless other outlets reported that the singe "Royals" had sold 85,000 copies in the US a mere three weeks after its release.

With "Royals" having done so well and "Tennis Court" seemingly primed to be as successful, Lorde's label and management felt it was time for the youngster to fly to the States and do a full-blown promotion blitz that, as the itinerary came together, would include television appearances, a handful of concerts and more interviews than she could shake a stick at.

Lorde was excited and a bit nervous at the tour which would commence in August. With so much to do in the next few weeks, she pretty much decided to take it easy and be Ella for a bit before she would go back to playing pop star.

On one of those nights off, Ella was in Auckland, partying with some friends and having no particular plans for the rest of the weekend . . . .When her phone suddenly buzzed. It was a frantic text from her manager. Maclachlan hastily explained that he had just received an equally frantic phone call from the promoter of the Splendor in the Grass music festival, an annual three day outdoor music festival that, that year, was being held at Yelgun near Byron Bay in New South Wales. Lorde was aware that the festival had been going on and would conclude in two days.

What she was about to find out was that one of her true musical idols, Frank Ocean, who was set to perform on the final day, had damaged his vocal chords and would be unable to perform. The promoters wanted to know if she would step in at the last minute to perform on that final day. With her friends screaming and hollering in the background, Lorde contemplated this out-of-nowhere request.

"I got the text on Friday at about 11:30," she recalled in a feature in *The Vine*. "I read the text and then just sort of left it. I wasn't thinking straight or something."

Finally, after a round of phone calls and texts to Lorde's parents, her bandmates and another call to Lorde, the singer finally got the picture. To jump in and replace one of her idols sounded too good to be true. There could be only one answer.

"I said okay," she recalled to the *Australian*.

But the craziness was far from over. Jimmy, a very hung-over Ben and Lorde got together for a quick rehearsal the next day. The set list had already been worked to death in preparation for the trip to the States, so that was not a problem. And Jimmy and Ben had recently purchased some new equipment that they were anxious to try out. Everything seemed in place for this impromptu gig as they hopped a plane in Auckland and headed for New South Wales.

On the flight down, Lorde reflected on the last minute gig. It would be the perfect busman's holiday. She was able to fine-tune her performing chops in front of 10,000 fans. That would be her most high-profile performance to date and only her third live show as Lorde was not lost on her. By the time the plane landed and the group were in their hotel, the nerves were beginning to set it. Lorde was confident.

But she also had a sudden case of the jitters.

Lorde and the band arrived at the festival site three and a half hours before they were due to go on. First they were awed by the size of the place and the literally thousands of people who were packed close to the front of the stage. When they finally arrived backstage and Lorde saw the caliber of performers wandering around, her confidence turned to mush.

"James Blake is wondering around backstage," she

recounted in *The Vine*. "Alt J is in the dressing room next to me. And I was like, 'Oh my God! What am I doing here?'"

Maclachlan could see that his charge was bordering on stage fright and, with a bit more than two hours before she was scheduled to perform, he suggested that Lorde wander about the festival grounds and just relax. Maclachlan explained to *The Vine* how quickly that plan backfired.

"So we went out and took about thirty steps and then she looked at me. I was like 'Are you okay?' And she said, 'I think I'd better go back.' There were people recognizing her, nudging, staring, double-taking, pointing. It was, like, 'Woah! Let's go back and chill out and then do the show."

Shortly after 5:30 pm, Lorde hit the stage. She still appeared uneasy. But then the band started pumping out her trademark haunting rhythms. The singer felt the stage fright slowly melting away.

"I don't really know how to explain what was going on in my head," she recounted that moment to *The Vine*. "I've got this blank part of my memory because I don't think I've ever been more terrified. I was like 'This is it. I've got to do it. I can do it now.'"

The crowd began to chant her name. The vibe was definitely supportive. Tension was replaced by calmness.

Lorde was now in complete control.

She came across as poised and polished, roaming the stage in an oh-so subtle fashion, projecting an image of contemplative exploration and excitement amid moments in which she played to the audience with a young girl's passion.

The only downside to this surprise performance was that Lorde had wanted to do a Frank Ocean song in tribute to the performer she replaced. Unfortunately, the call to perform was so last minute that she did not have time to rehearse a tune.

But that blemish was more than compensated for by the fact that, according to Maclachlan in *The Vine*, her third show as a performer had proved an important point. "I think what the Splendor performance did was confirm that Ella can do it live in front of a crowd of ten to fifteen thousand. That's a big call."

Lorde's coming out live on a large scale also appealed to the fan in her as she was in a lineup- that included a personal favorite, James Blake, and such hip acts as Of Monsters and Men and Gurrumul.

When she came off the stage, Lorde was smiling. It was a moment of triumph captured in time.

It would have been the perfect send off to her trip to the United States . . .

. . . If it wasn't for the pain.

CHAPTER TEN

COMING TO AMERICA

"I came down with a kidney infection just as I was about to get on the plane," she told *The Telegraph*. "They took me to the hospital and put me on a drip and now I'm on heavy antibiotics."

The kidney infection would clear itself up but the result of the antibiotics was that, for a number of days, Lorde would have trouble sitting upright. Consequently she was not in the greatest of spirits as she prepared to board the plane for America. Her physical discomfort was meshing uneasily with her erratic emotional state. She was not sure how well she would sleep on the transatlantic flight and so she brought along a bottle of Nyquil to help her doze during the flight.

Lorde had never flown on a plane in her life until the puddle jump to the festival. And so as she went up the gangway and into the plane, there was most likely a little bit of nerves, because America was many hours and 9,000 miles away. But with her older sister Jerry along on the trip to chaperone, her bandmates and her manager, the nerves were most likely replaced by the excitement of this next and all-important phase of her career.

Spreading the gospel of Lorde in America.

This trip was set up as a preliminary first strike, an August

6 show at New York's hip Le Poisson Rouge and a quick cross-country hop to Los Angeles and a much anticipated show at The Echoplex. This would be a fairly heavy industry trip, a meet and greet with record company executives and industry heavyweights. Lots of press and lots of happy talk loomed on the horizon. If anybody Lorde's age managed to get into the show that night in New York, it would be more by chance than design. In a sense, Lorde had a lot to prove with this first trip across the pond.

Yes "Royals" and *The Love Club* EP had been selling like the proverbial hot cakes and Lorde had recently captured the honor of being the first female performer in seventeen years to top the *Billboard* Alternate Rock Charts. Lorde's reaction to the news was typical of how a normal teenager would take things. Her initial reaction was to be "cool" about it. But, as witness her reaction in *Billboard*, "cool" quickly dissolved into glee. "It feels like a combination of my birthday, Christmas and washing my hair after a month of not doing so."

But to the US record sales and chart listings did not mean a lot at that point. Lorde was still largely a mystery. Her music was an original force of nature. But how would Lorde go down in a live setting? It remained to be seen.

An amusing aside to the trip was the alterations that had to be made to accommodate the age and legality of Lorde in a time honored music lifestyle that was traditionally geared toward adults. One concession that she jokingly explained in an NPR interview was the exclusion of any alcoholic beverages in the singer's backstage refreshment rider. "Another was the fact that the hotel staff would go into my room and clean out the mini bar before I got there."

Lorde made the most of her short time in New York to do

a bit of touring and take in the sights and, in a *Huffington Post* interview, related that it was definitely her kind of place.

"New York is crazy. It's pretty overwhelming and it's so busy. But everything just seems to fit there."

Lorde would recall in a conversation with *Spin* that there was a sense of déjà vu, experiencing a New York that she had long seen in movies and television shows... But she thrived on the fact that the city was so alien to anything she had experienced in New Zealand.

"I had such a good time," she said. "I didn't have time to do anything really amazing because I had to work. But I did a photo shoot on the top of the Empire State Building that was both tourism and promotion."

And it was in New York that the singer discovered how well "Royals" had traveled in advance of her first US appearance. Fans she did not know she had turned out to meet her at the airport and were camping out outside her hotel. For a relative unknown, it was like Biebermania

"Which was weird," she chuckled at the memory in conversation with *The Guardian*. "People at the airport. You're like, really cool."

It was also a moment when Lorde found out that she had suddenly become the darling of the celebrity set. Selena Gomez and R. Kelly were among the A list celebrities who courted her with quick hellos and tweet congratulations on her good fortune. And in a gesture that left her totally amazed and amused, she received a not-too-veiled offer from the already nostalgic Backstreet Boys to collaborate with her on a song.

After only three shows together, Lorde and her bandmates were still getting to know each other personally and professionally. From the beginning, Jimmy and Ben's ease in working behind somebody much younger than them who was basically calling all the shots was a plus. Their chemistry was further strengthened by the fact that they had the same musical tastes and sense of humor. That they were all up for eating often and, occasionally, exotically didn't hurt either. Jimmy and Ben quickly became her older and highly protective brothers. They had been around music long enough to always be aware of what Ella was up to at all times, aided and abetted by her manager and sister.

Their pre-performance ritual came quite naturally as Lorde explained in a *Rookie Magazine* interview.

"Usually I need a couple of minutes by myself," she declared. "I warm up and I stride around the room in different, weird ways. Then I do body warm-ups because there's nothing worse than getting on stage and being all non-limber. Then we just listen to a couple of songs, me and my band, and I just sing and move around. I'm quite a hand-mover onstage, so I let that side of me come out pre-show."

But there was something else Lorde had to contend with the night of her appearance at Le Poisson Rogue. Sitting backstage in her dressing room, surrounded by her family, band members, sister and manager, Lorde was feeling decidedly out of sorts. Part of it continued to be the effects of the antibiotics, part of it was jet lag that refused to catch up with the fact that she was more than 9,000 miles away from home. She was putting up a good front but it was easy to spot that the young singer was a little rough around the edges. But, much like she had pulled it together in the Splendor in the Grass festival, Lorde pulled it together when the house lights went down.

Lorde took the New York stage that first night amid an air of excitement and anticipation. There was the sense of high drama that only the singer could project. During the midpoint in her rendition of "Tennis Court," her too cool, other worldly demeanor was suddenly punctuated by a smile and a dip of her head in acknowledgement of the audience. Perhaps sensing that she had strayed too far from her persona, she suddenly whipped her hair around and returned her to a nonchalant if sometimes spooky appearing stance. Songs like "Royals" and "Bravado" resonated with lyrical and musical light and shadows.

At one point in the show, as chronicled by a *Billboard* review, she addressed the audience, saying, "I'm so humbled to be here." It was a symbolic moment to say the least. Figuratively Lorde had taken her first plane ride . . .

And she had arrived safely.

Lorde winged her way across country to Los Angeles where she found a different kind of vibe. To her way of thinking, the tone of the city was different from New York and just a little bit weird. "There was this huge picture of giant breasts above my bed," she told *The Huffington Post*. "I got there and it was like, 'Man! I have definitely arrived in LA.'"

And she took what little time she had to be the prototypical tourist as only somebody new to Hollywood could be. In a 97.1 AMP conversation, she gushed that she was "staying in the coolest hotel" and that she had a constant giggle as she walked down Hollywood Boulevard and saw the more infamous 'adults only' establishments. One in particular, Looks of Love would be pasted in her permanent mental memory book.

The hip music crowd in Los Angeles had been waiting with open arms. The Echoplex was a small standing-room-only club. Consequently the show easily sold out with ticket prices climbing to as much as $120.

That was the upside to the trip to Los Angeles. But the

down side remained the crippling stage fright that was her constant companion right up to the moment where she hit the stage. In a candid conversation with *The Australian*, Lorde explained the real horrors of touring.

"Before I go onstage, I lock into this period of the most crippling fear. It's something I wouldn't wish on somebody I hated. It's the worst half hour of my life, every night. But then it gets replaced by something magic."

And true to her prediction, the moment the lights went down, the fear melted away.

With a more youthful, less music industry audience, Lorde felt an immediate connection and was in complete control during a brief forty five minute set in which she trotted out just about everything on *The Love Club* EP, as well as some new material.

Lorde took the occasion of the Los Angeles stopover to announce that her first full album, entitled *Pure Heroine*, would have its official unveiling on September 27 and would contain "Royals," "Tennis Court" and eight brand new songs.

During her brief stay in Los Angeles, Lorde also experienced her first real life encounter with a rabid pack of paparazzi that snapped pictures of the young singer as she was standing outside a restaurant. In the aftermath of the encounter, she speculated that being stalked by paparazzi was part of the price she would have to pay now that she was somebody famous.

Lorde also found time to make an almost prerequisite appearance on *The Kevin and Bean Show* on trend-setting radio station KROQ where she performed "Royals" live in the studio and patently, and with much good humor, answered the expected questions that were now on the verge of getting old, but were not quite there yet.

While in Los Angeles, Lorde began what would be regular appearances on the daytime and nighttime talk show circuit, singing "Royals' on *The Ellen Show*. For Lorde this was pretty simple stuff. Ellen introduced Lorde. Lorde sang "Royals" and then Ellen hugs Lorde and the show fades to commercial. Quick and dirty but it got the point across. Lorde was now a viable act in front of Middle America.

And what she was finding along the way was a line of questioning that, by this time was evolving well beyond the "What's your favorite color" teen magazine clichés People seemed interested in her in a much more serious way. Of course there were the expected questions of how she got to be Lorde, which she typically answered with patience and no small sense of humor.

But the more serious music press was willing to ask her about the more serious aspects of her music. Feminism remained high on the list of media questions. So did the sorry state of pop music and the perceived notion of Lorde as the anti-Katy Perry and Justin Bieber who was out to singlehandedly save pop from itself.

"For so long, pop music has been a super shameful thing," she told MTV with no small amount of candor. "But the way I see it, pop music doesn't have to be stupid and alternative music doesn't have to be boring. People have a brain and I think you can combine saying something clever with saying something in a highly accessible way."

Lorde returned home on the wings of triumph. The day of her New York debut had also signaled an announcement that "Royals" had become the most shared track by a new artist in 2013. She would also discover that the song she had once considered an afterthought had quickly crossed over into 'classic' status which meant that it was suddenly one of the most covered songs on the planet with literally hundreds of takes on the song, by artists with varying degrees of notoriety, appearing in online and the occasional live version. Among the more well -known artists to take their turn at "Royals" were Selena Gomez, Saints of Victory, The Weekend, and Gap 5.

Hoping for a bit of rest and relaxation, Lorde quickly found that the next few weeks were wall to wall interview obligations, last minute studio time to fine tune *Pure Heroine* in advance of its September 27 unveiling and fulfilling a long held promise to do her first live show in the UK.

The irony of that show, at London's famed Madame Jojos, was that the club was an adults-only, eighteen and older venue and that Lorde was not yet old enough to buy a ticket. The UK is traditionally a tough market to crack but once on your side, these music lovers can be fanatic in their support. The sold-out show indicated how quickly Lorde had become a British fave and the singer, based on reviews of the show, rewarded the audience with a solid performance that showcased the ease in which Lorde's vocals had meshed with the very sparse modern pop musical backing.

It would be the ideal send up to her second, six city assault on the States set to begin September 25 and to coincide with the September 27 release of *Pure Heroine.*

The Belasco Theater in downtown Los Angeles was an immediate step up from the cramped Echoplex show from her previous trip. And by this time, it was apparent that Lorde had been a quick study in how to please her fans in a live setting. Starting out moody in an under lit stage, the performance turned lighthearted and fan-friendly as Lorde's between-song audience patter effectively showed her as quite human and, yes, still a young woman amid the sudden rush of stardom.

The show concluded with the stage once again going dark and the singer quite literally disappearing off stage, not to return despite a five-minute chorus of "encore" from the audience. The sense among those in attendance was that she probably would have done the encore if, in a bit more than an hour set, she had not sung every song she knew. The *Belasco* show had been such an immediate sell-out that Lorde readily agreed to do a second show the following day at The Fonda Theater, which would also sell out.

That these shows were selling out so quickly was not lost on the tour company and management. Lorde readily agreed to filling in the days off with additional shows at selected stops. The immediate sellout of the upcoming Webster Hall date in New York resulted in a second sold out show in the same venue being added. And when that wasn't enough to accommodate the mania for the singer, a third date was added the following day at the Warsaw in Brooklyn. The one Canadian show, the 700-seat Hoxton in Toronto, had sold out so quickly that the promoters immediately found a larger alternative in the 1,427 seat Danforth Theater Hall which would, likewise, be filled to capacity when Lorde hit the stage.

The Fillmore show in San Francisco on September 27 was memorable for a lot of reasons. *Pure Heroine* was being released that day so there was that sense of anticipation. The Fillmore had hosted countless legendary performers over the years and for Lorde to perform in those hallowed halls was something not lost on the sixteen year old. The show itself had evolved into a manageable hour plus set with everything from *The Love Club* and selections from *Pure Heroine t*o prime the pump. What the audience had not counted on was a surprise when Lorde, unexpectedly broke into the as-yet unreleased song "Good Fights." It was the definition of a haunting, moody modern pop performance that had the reviewer from the *San Jose Mercury News* making favorable comparisons between the likes of Tori Amos, Amy Winehouse and Adele.

The singer did yet another live studio performance of "Royals" on that bastion of liberal leanings and creative attitudes, radio station KCRW. Although in a relative cocoon of promotion and performing, Lorde was still finding time to speak her mind and to be controversial.

Around the time of The Fillmore performance, comments she had recently made during a *GQ Q* blog were going viral thanks to the internet and such outlets as *The Huffington Post* and the *San Jose Mercury News* in which she defended her normalcy by taking some shots at the pre-fab Disney created performers.

"The difference between those kids and me is that I grew up completely normal and went to parties and had that experience. I'm much less inclined to be like, 'Look! I'm fucking mental!'"

Lorde's participation in The Decibel Festival, a decade-long Seattle, Washington tradition in which DJ's and progressive musicians perform in various sized venues all across the city, brought out an assured and passionate performance, seemingly giving new life and edge to her songs each time she sang them. A bonus on this particular night was Lorde showing her admiration for Kanye West by surprising the packed Showbox Market Club with a raw rendition of West's, "Hold My Liquor."

The added dates in New York allowed Lorde the time to stretch her legs a bit and, on one night, she was spotted hanging out at a local billiard bar with some friends. But the reality was that, like it or not, being sixteen and underage in a city like New York, she was never really alone as she candidly said in an interview with *The Associated Press*.

"Every time I go out, it's with my mum and my band and my manager," she said, sounding very much like the teen who was craving just a little bit of freedom. "I have all these adults looking over me so, honestly, it's all pretty tame."

Lorde's final performance at The Davenport Theater Hall in Toronto, Canada was, on the surface, a near carbon copy of the previous shows. She had grown as a live performer in a matter of days, owning the stage and pushing her lyrical and musical influences to the limit and beyond. But reportedly those who were at that last show on the tour saw that little something extra. The emotions, in her vocals and in her lyrics seemed to have an extra coat of tension and emotion to them. She was not prowling the stage as an effect but rather with a true purpose. With this final stop on this mini-tour, Lorde had suddenly emerged from her on-the-job training as a pop star in waiting . . .

. . . And was heading for bigger and better things.

CHAPTER ELEVEN

HEROINE BECOMES PURE

August 12, 2013. This tweet from Joel Little pretty much said it all. "Album's all done. Am away next week."

Although the official unveiling would not be until September 27, 2013, *Pure Heroine* was officially in the can at that point. Of course there were those months leading up to Joel's tweet to consider.

Which included the question of whether Lorde would be allowed to take what amounted to three months off from her normal life and, particularly, school to do the album. She admitted to *The Music* that there were some anxious moments in that regard.

"It was pretty much down to my parents because, obviously, I would have to take three months out of school. They came home from a meeting with my manager and said, 'we're going to let you make the record.' I was like, 'Yeah, this is going to be awesome!'"

And in typical Lorde fashion, a task so simple as naming the album took some long and lingering thought. Lorde knew that with the title *Pure Heroine* she would be setting herself up for all sorts of drug implications and that the title was ripe for double entendre. But as she was quick to point out in an interview with *3rd Degree*, it was much more simple than that.

"I've always had this thing about liking how words looked on the page as well as how they sounded. That's basically how I chose the title. I've never been one to think in terms of double entendre."

Shortly after the completion of *The Love Club* EP, Lorde was already making plans for her first full-length album. And although she would occasionally express the desire to someday work with other producers, it was a foregone conclusion that the chemistry developed between Lorde and Joel was a bond that would not, or could not, be broken.

The singer jokingly said as much in conversation with *Discus*. "Joel is the official producer (of the album). We often don't see eye to eye, but I always get what I want at the end of the day."

Lorde had rounded into a very prolific songwriter in the preceding months and so, not surprisingly, there were quite a few songs available for the album. In fact, at final count, there were seventeen songs, all quite album-worthy about the time Lorde and Joel entered his studio to begin the recording process. But it was determined, with no small suggestion from Maclachlan, that ten songs were considered the industry standard for an album. It was also determined that, despite the fact that two of those songs were already worldwide hits, that two of the songs on the album should be "Royals" and "Tennis Court." What remained for Lorde were eight songs that would be determined by a rapidly evolving pallet of sounds and emotions.

Musically Lorde was insistent that *Pure Heroine* would revolve around some already established elements. It would be her voice, in that haunting, brooding and observational way that would carry the load. Lyrically her takes on the life of teens she knew and how she perceived it would continue to anchor the proceedings. In that way she has of explaining things, Lorde told *Discus* how she saw *Pure Heroine* as more of the same but different.

"The goal for me was to make a body of work that was cohesive," she said. "If I can make something that feels like that and feels right and true and good then I will have succeeded."

Lorde's approach to *Pure Heroine* translated into an even more progressive sound in the studio which meant that Lorde and Joel would be burning the midnight oil and that experimentation would be the order of the day.

The mercurial singer would later admit that, despite having a solid basis in what she wanted the album to sound like, she really did not have anything specific in mind. Lorde had been listening to a lot of hip-hop and electronic music of late and had been channeling James Blake and Lana Del Rey for a specific kind of vibe. But at the end of the day, it all boiled down to Lorde and Joel amid the confines of Golden Age Studios.

As with *The Love Club* and *Tennis Court* EP's, the *Pure Heroine* sessions were conspicuous by their minimalism. A literal skeleton crew of musicians was on hand to supplement and explore Joel's electronic beats, loops and all manner of trickery. Joel was quickly becoming the master of the form and the result on *Pure Heroine* was a sound that was even more dark and shadowy than Lorde's previous music.

That the singer's voice was more than a one trick gimmick was born out in the way Lorde's vocal range moved freely and often in a highly progressive manner throughout the songs. Her voice as an instrument of contemplation in several forms was much in evidence on the song "Ribs" before turning light and airy on "Buzzcut Season." For Lorde, *Pure Heroine* was an exercise in earthiness and constraint but fully capable of darting all over the vocal highway in an often surreal manner.

Lyrically her songwriting continued to evolve. The themes of exploring teen angst, love and just being sixteen and getting through the day was, if anything, more sharp and focused. In the best possible sense, Lorde had adopted a take-no-prisoners attitude in her songwriting that continued to make valid thought provoking and existential points. Lorde was definitely flexing intellectual muscles and the result was a giant step forward.

On the same day Joel made his Twitter announcement, Lorde followed up with one of her own, likewise announcing that the album was done and would be released September 27.

Rather than jubilation at the reality that her debut album was about to meet the masses, Lorde suddenly and unexpectedly found herself in a state of depression. She explained the mental and emotional collapse to *Rookie Magazine*.

"It was terrifying," she recalled. "In the months leading up to putting the album out, I was sleeping really badly, maybe three or four hours a night. I was a mess. I asked myself why I was having these problems and what was wrong with me? And I finally realized that I was terrified about giving this part of myself to other people."

Lorde would get over this fear as only Lorde could, logically coming to the conclusion that, once she went through the process of creating the songs and putting them out there, they were no longer hers.

Needless to say, Universal Music Group knew that the album had the potential to be a worldwide smash and so threw a massive amount of money and marketing acumen into promoting the eminent arrival of *Pure Heroine*; much of which borrowed from the DIY magic that Lorde had worked on *The Love Club*. The song "Ribs" was given away free on I Tunes a week before the release of the album to prime the pump. The first single from the album, "Team" was made available world-wide on September 13.

Upon release, *Pure Heroine* proved an across the board critical smash. *Billboard* acknowledged the album as "immaculate, and Lorde the most vocally striking and lyrically thought provoking artist in recent times." *3 News* said the album "'lives up to the hype and exceeds expectations." *The Dominion Post* was one of the few naysayers allowing as "the album was not groundbreaking and did not offer any surprises" but conceded that "it was gold and a strong debut."

"Team" would prove a worthy follow up to Lorde's singles' hit parade, debuting at No. 3 on the New Zealand Singles Charts and climbing to No.8 on the all- important *Billboard* Singles Charts and marking Lorde's third top-ten position on the *Billboard* listings.

Likewise *Pure Heroine* crashed the charts in a hurry. The album would debut at No.1 on the New Zealand album charts and would be certified platinum in record time. *Pure Heroine* would have a bit of a rougher go on the *Billboard* Top 200 Album Charts. After debuting at No. 3 with 129,000 copies sold that first week, *Pure Heroine* would drop over the next two weeks to No.7 before rebounding to No.5. The album would be certified gold in the States by Christmas.

Amid the critical praise and Lorde's continuing attitude of not holding back in interviews, it would eventually be revealed that the singer had a mystery collaborator as she explained in an extensive interview with *The Cut*.

...work accompanying the release of the song "Royals", one of the first images ass...
...his song for Lorde's free download. SOUNDCLOUD.COM. UNDER LICENSE FROM CREATIVE...

A promotional studio glamour shot. FELIXJTAPIA.ORG, UNDER LICENSE FROM CREATIVE COMMONS

Lorde wearing Chanel at the Museum of Modern Art celebration in New York City where she rubbed elbows with David Bowie and Tilda Swinto. DIGGITA.IT, UNDER FROM CREATIVE COMMONS

Lorde performing "Royals" at KCRW. FELIX.JTAPIA ORG, UNDER LICENSE FROM CREATIVE COMMONS

Lorde in her Grammy-wining performance. POPCRUSH.COM, UNDER LICENSE FROM CREATIVE COMMONS

Lorde and her boyfriend James Lowe share a moment away from the public.

Lorde and new BFF Taylor Swift after her Grammy win.

At one point she took the lyrics to her boyfriend, photographer James Lowe, and showed them to him. She explained that sharing things with her boyfriend encouraged much of the album's writing and ultimately inspired and drove her to write the majority of the album.

So it was finally revealed that Lorde had a boyfriend. Now the question remained . . .

. . . Who was James Lowe?

CHAPTER TWELVE

MEET THE BOYFRIEND

James Lowe is a twenty-four year-old photographer who hails from Devenport in New Zealand. He is tall, lanky, wears glasses and projects a boyish, somewhat geeky look. It is only an afterthought that James Lowe is Asian. He was a friend of Lorde's when she was still Ella. He was a friend of Ella's before fate and talent stepped in to make her a star.

Today James Lowe is the true love of Lorde's life.

By the time Lorde turned seventeen late in 2013, word had pretty much gotten out that Lorde was involved with a much older man. Her parents had been cautious at the idea of their daughter dating somebody seven years her senior but when they met him, they came away feeling that he was a nice boy and a good intellectual match for their daughter. Lorde's very first relationship, some years prior to getting involved with James, was with a boy four years older than her. That Lorde was mature beyond her years almost made it inevitable that she would be attracted to older men.

It's interesting to note that, in her choice of men, Lorde, like her music, has run contrary to the prevailing notion of hooking up with one's own peers in the industry. And rather than sharing the spotlight with another ego-driven performer and having their every moment chronicled in the tabloids,

Lorde has gone the other way when it comes to romance.

James is truly creative but, perhaps because he's a photographer, has willingly been supportive yet behind the scenes. He has been amazingly attentive to her needs, has the same interests in art, culture and music and traveled in the same circles. Those who had witnessed the growing relationship between the pair most likely approved. Because James was quite simply too good to be true. James was there for all of her shows and important events. And he is a true romantic. In a recent *People* article, snippets from James' website offered true evidence of his feelings toward Lorde,

"Still no words . . . So proud." "I'm happy today . . . She's amazing."

Given her admittedly introverted nature it is nothing sort of a miracle that the pair got together as she explained in a *Daily Entertainment News* article. "I'm quite solitary by nature. I don't have heaps and heaps of friends. Often I can appreciate a place regardless of the people I'm sharing it with."

James had turned out to be the ideal sharing companion, especially in the quiet contemplative moments that Lorde craved. She explained to *Daily Entertainment News* what James' companionship has meant to her creative life.

"James and I spent a lot of time driving around all over our city and that for me was enlightening," she recalled, "because, for once, the company that I was keeping was effecting how I was feeling about those places and in a positive way. I think that was kind of what drove me to write a lot of the stuff on *Pure Heroine*. I really thought about where I was in conjunction with who I was with."

Although their relationship had been kept fairly low profile for some time, pictures of the pair frolicking in swimsuits at a beach came to light in October 2013 on an international celebrity gossip site that finally brought their relationship fully to the public eye. Lorde and James thought nothing of it. But other people did.

David Grr, a Facebook and Instagram operator, had gathered a respectable 26,000 followers. When he happened upon those initial photos, he thought nothing of reposting one of them. But Grr recalled in a *Herald on Sunday* conversation "things just kind of got out of hand."

The Internet was suddenly bombarded with hateful tweets directed at Lorde and, in particular, James. Some, as reported in *Rolling Stone,* and *US* were as the result of Lorde's public disregard for the boy band One Direction. But many others were particularly hateful in tone and downright racist.

"What the fuck is Lorde and that Chinese sort of ostrich anyway," read one. "Girl, your boyfriend looks like Mao Tse Tung," read another. "Lorde's boyfriend looks like the Chinese exchange student from *Sixteen Candles*," blasted another.

Lorde would recall the incident in *Rookie*. "Suddenly there were, like. hundreds of people from my city looking at my picture and making fun of me." The attacks would also bring back recent but bitter memories of being teased for wearing weird clothes and reading weird books.

Lorde was extremely upset by the remarks and took it upon herself to track down Grr through his Facebook account and told Grr that he was cruel to expose her to those kinds of attacks. Grr would apologize and immediately removed the photo. But he did not go quietly, telling *Herald on Sunday* that he had essentially done her a favor by exposing her relationship to the world.

"If she takes everything personally, she's going to be a wreck by the end of the year," he said. "I had to say something to her, as a warning to her, that she needed to harden up a little bit."

Things would seem to have truly gotten a bit out of control when a fellow performer, Tyler: The Creator posted an Instagram video mocking the young couple. Surprisingly Lorde's response was that it made her laugh.

But in quieter moments she would acknowledge that while she was a celebrity, she was also quite human and hinted that the attacks on James and herself had been upsetting.

If Lorde was upset by the attacks, she tended to put her anger aside in favor of amazement and circumspect responses as she recalled in *Rolling Stone*.

"That was some pretty weird shit," she recalled. "You almost wonder about humans. Walking around Auckland, it's easy to notice that it's a diverse city with lots of interracial-relationships. That's why the reaction came as such a surprise to me. No one I know would even think this was a big deal."

Lorde would ultimately be proven right as, after the initial blast from the haters, the furor quite simply went away. Pictures of Lorde and James walking hand in hand and posing for funny cell phone photos became more and more common. The pair was not hiding anything.

Quite simply they were young and in love.

And at the end of the day, he was the ideal man to support his woman. Because into September 2013, things were about to get even busier for the woman whose popularity on a worldwide scale was growing by leaps and bounds.

Which, indirectly, made Lorde and James' life a bit more difficult as the singer lamented in a thoughtful, introspective essay that appeared in *Sunday Magazine*.

"Sometimes my boyfriend and I get photographed on the street when we just want to have time that doesn't belong to other people."

CHAPTER THIRTEEN

COME SEPTEMBER

Lorde would tell anybody who asked that she was truly in control of what was going on in her career. But by September, with her music selling in the millions and her time being more and more occupied by promotion and press, even she had those moments when she felt that what she created was now not entirely her own.

"I feel completely in control," she insisted in a wide-ranging interview with *3rd Degree*. "Although even at some points people seem to be trying to get control. But at the end of the day, it's my art and I'm in control."

The control Lorde was speaking of may well have been the growing hype generated by an all too willing press. Superlatives were falling like rain, much of it admittedly justified. The most persistent being that Lorde was almost certainly a lock for at least four Grammy nominations at the upcoming awards program. Lorde tended to take those kinds of pronouncements with a grain of salt, pointing to her lifelong sense of perfectionism as a defense against believing her own press.

"I feel like I constantly have to prove myself because of my age," she told *3rd Degree*.

However, even with the ever-growing notoriety, Lorde acknowledged to *Fader* that she was still a bit below the radar despite the hit records, the shows and a mountain of press. "I'm still not like very famous and I definitely have a very private life. It's only been six or eight months since I released *The Love Club* EP and since people had any idea who I was. So I've been able to have a fairly normal time of things."

Proving herself at this point meant doing the business side of music and doing yet another round of promotion and a handful of concerts. A second return to the States had been scheduled to begin late in September but Lorde was taking the time to grease the wheels on her side of the Pacific as well. Her *3rd Degree* interview in New Zealand would prove a straightforward and revealing look at how Lorde was dealing with the stardom.

Lorde followed with an appearance on the legendary music show *Later . . . With Jools Holland*. It was an all-star line up to kick off the show's seventeenth season that included The Kings of Leon and Lorde's longtime idol Kanye West. The singer recalled in *Rolling Stone* how she was quite literally a giggling little girl upon the occasion of meeting Kanye.

"He shook my hand and said he liked the messages in my songs," she related. "I was saying to myself 'Keep cool. This is normal.'"

Sensing that "Royals" and "Tennis Court" had pretty much played out their potential as hit singles, Lorde announced that her third single "Team" would be available on September 13. Although the song was part of the *Pure Heroine* album, it became evident that this was Lorde, lyrically and emotionally, growing a bit older.

A haunting hybrid of pop, rock and electro pop, the song is also forthright in taking on the notion of teen rebellion, how important it ultimately is and how we all, at some point, must get on with our lives. It was a by-product of Lorde's sudden introduction to a much bigger world and an encouraging sign that Lorde could effectively grow with her sound and attitude.

The "Team" video, directed by Alex Takacs aka Young Replicant, was, by comparison to the previous two videos, a much more ambitious and literal *Lord of the Flies* story in which a young boy travels to an island populated by teens and partakes in various tests to determine if he is worthy of joining them. From its inception, the "Team" video carried the banner of art and alienation. Although Young Replicant was more than capable of directing the proceedings, it was an unwritten role that Lorde, for everything from the casting of 'different looking' teens to the visual style, had the final say so. The director admitted to MTV that the singer and he went back and forth on various elements of the shoot before Lorde ultimately got her way.

The headstrong singer would insist that Lorde's rule was law in an MTV feature. "Basically everything that I put out that has my name on it is controlled by me. I have a very strong visual identity. I know how I want stuff to look. I'm almost too involved."

Lorde flew back to the States at the end of September to begin her second US trek. The first stop was the *Late Night with Jimmy Fallon* show. Viewers were expecting yet another rendition of "Royals" which they got. But what came as a surprise was an encore of the haunting and poignant "White Teeth Teens" off the *Pure Heroine* album.

The song was not considered a candidate for singles stardom and so not necessarily something to be showcased on US television. But Lorde wanted to do it, so who was to argue? There was another quick stop on *The Ellen Show* and another round of "Royals" before Lorde would once again put her talent to the test in another concert setting.

The Warsaw Theater in Brooklyn, New York had been considered a bastion for Polish culture. That Lorde would headline a concert there was not lost on the singer who, according to a *Complex* review, turned to the sold-out audience at one point and acknowledged, "This is really weird." In reality what the show would turn out to be was a barometer of where Lorde was in the pop music world.

The concert showcased the singer as a first rate performer who had long since gotten her stage legs and was presenting her persona in a well-defined manner. And, as with all performers who have 'arrived' in such a spectacular manner, the question remained, what was next?

That's when Hollywood came calling. The Hunger Games film series was already considered a blockbuster movie franchise and the bottom line people felt that there was no better way to increase the *The Hunger Games: Catching Fire* prospects than with an all-star soundtrack by a wildly divergent lineup of current pop stars. Lorde immediately came to mind as did the potential of a cover of the Tears for Fears classic "Everybody Wants to Rule the World". Lorde readily accepted the offer, feeling there was something she could do with the song that would make it different. And in her hands, the classic piece of pop history suddenly became very much her own, an extremely brooding and dirge-like call to war that fit perfectly into her realm of contemplative music. The feeling was that Lorde would most likely include the reworked chestnut on an upcoming album.

Lorde hopscotched back across the Pacific to keep a long held promise. Australia had been particularly supportive early on and had, for a long time, been begging for a live show. Lorde went that request one better when she scheduled four shows between October 16-21 in Brisbane, Sydney, Canaberra and Melbourne in conjunction with the release of *Pure Heroine* in that country.

The shows were highly successful on all fronts. The shows were also conspicuous by the question most often asked by audience members who, to a person, seemed amazed that a girl so young could be such a talented and polished performer.

Just before beginning her Australian mini-tour, Lorde and Joel received a very special local honor when 10,000 New Zealand songwriters, a branch of the Australian Performing Rights Association, voted the pair the coveted Silver Scroll Award for "Royals".. This was a pivotal moment for Lorde as it was the first award she received for creativity rather than sales.

As reported by *The Music Network*, the pair shared a humorous and emotional moment on stage when Joel turned to Lorde and said "It's taken me ten years to get up on this stage and it's taken you ten months. You're so annoying. The scary part is that you definitely haven't written your best song yet."

Lorde returned to New Zealand where the days leading up to her seventeenth birthday were filled with preparations for upcoming tours as well as the occasional very quick foray into the studio.

The woman would prove particularly astute when it came to merchandising her name. She definitely had opinions about what posters should look like and what kind of illustrations should appear on T-shirts and other clothing. Like everything else in her worldview, even the more crass commercial world would fall to her artistic visions.

This all spells money for Lorde as does just about everything she has done over the past year and change. But suddenly having more money than she's ever dreamed of having, with more on the way, has been somewhat daunting for the singer. With her finances being watched over by her father, Lorde has still had more money to play around with.

But she has been slow to coming out of her frugal shell. She has regularly said that even a purchase of $200 gives her pause and that she is not the type to blow her money on big cars and houses, but would rather buy geeky things like first edition books and old records And she just shrugs and smiles when reporters indicate that she is most likely already worth several million dollars at the ripe old age of seventeen. That did not mean as much to her as the idea that the money had truly been the result of her creativity and passion.

Lorde flew back to the States in early November for another round of promotion. A particular stop on the nighttime talk show *The Late Show with David Letterman* cemented her celebrity in America. Rather than do "Royals" again, Lorde indicated that she was already moving past the song when she chose to do her most recent single "Team" instead. But those who tuned into the show's webcast *Live with David Letterman* were happily surprised when the singer trotted out a veritable mini-concert that included not only "Royals" and the aforementioned "Team," but the songs "Bravado," "Tennis Court," "Buzzcut Season," "Ribs" and "White Teeth Teens."

Now more familiar with New York and its vibe, Lorde would spend the next few days in the Big Apple, celebrating her seventeenth birthday on November 7, amid family, friends and good cheer.

High on her list of memorable moments turning

seventeen was the invitation to perform at the Museum of Modern Art Film Benefit. It was a moment that she would be reluctant to talk about because it was just too personal to her. But she would offer to *The New Zealand Listener* that the night was a truly existential experience. "Performing at MOMA? That was just one of those moments in your life. It was like 'What am I doing here? How am I on this path?' It was just so incredible that I was jealous of myself."

She would do a high-powered rendition of "Royals" in front of a celebrity crowd that included benefit honoree, actress Tilda Swinton, legendary musician David Bowie, Ralph Fiennes, Drew Barrymore and designer Karl Lagerfeld. But for the pure fan, the meeting of Swinton and Bowie were the high points of the evening.

Lorde tweeted of the meeting with the actress, "I performed at the MOMA benefit honoring Tilda Swinton. Such an honor. That woman is phenomenal, a true heroine."

In conversation with Bowie she had to fight real hard against turning into a crazed fan. Initially Lorde had been reluctant to make this very personal moment public but eventually she relented in a conversation with *Rookie*.

"We were holding hands and staring into each other's eyes and talking. It was insane. A beautiful moment. To have somebody like David Bowie tell you that listening to you was like listening to tomorrow . . . It was like I could creatively die and be happy forever."

Also in town at the time was prize-winning New Zealand author Eleanor Catton. Lorde's mother had arranged for the two Kiwis to meet and they spent a good part of the night reminiscing and just talking as only two celebrated New Zealanders can.

However it wasn't all celebrity and glitz that night. Lorde wound down that evening with a rousing game of bowling at a local Brooklyn alley. There was also a small moment as she was being driven back to her hotel in a cab that she related in a tweet. "I was in a cab going home in New York City and 'Royals' came on the drivers' radio and I laughed. The driver asked why and I told him it was my song and he said 'mine too.'"

Lorde woke up from her amazing night to yet another present. "Royals" had been confirmed No. 1 on the *Billboard* US Charts for the sixth week in a row.

This being her first birthday away from home, and acknowledging that a lot had happened in her life in the past year, Lorde poured out her feelings and emotions on turning seventeen and suddenly being a star in a Tumblr letter that would also find a home in *Sunday Magazine*.

"I think back to my last birthday and how it fell in the middle of exam revision but a bunch of my friends came over anyway to eat cake and ruffle my hair and to talk about Pokémon (a game). Weirdoes. Miss them and my family terribly. But I have kind of a family here in New York. Our little tight bunch playing shows and being overwhelmed constantly and falling asleep in the backs of cabs."

During her time in New York, Lorde would also make a November 11 appearance at the VH-1 You Oughta' Know Concert at the Roseland Ballroom, a showcase of up and coming new talent. Yet another sign that the singer had, in the minds of those who dictated hip, arrived.

But it remained for her birthday present, on November 7, to put the capper on any notion that Lorde was not the real thing. Lorde signed a music publishing deal with Songs Music Publishing for a reported $2.5 million. The worldwide deal, according to *Billboard*, would include rights to *The Love Club* EP, *Pure Heroine* and all future recordings. It would also open up opportunities for Lorde to collaborate with other artists and write songs specifically for other people.

The competition for Lorde's publishing turned out to be a year-long process in which more than half a dozen of the biggest music publishing houses engaged in a heated bidding war for her music rights.

Lorde's manager recalled in a wide-ranging *Stuff* interview that he was "essentially spinning plates" during the year-long courtship of his client. He related that things got so heated that one suitor offered him the use of a private jet to go to meetings. And then, he recalled, there was the money being tossed around.

"She's been offered ridiculous amounts of money," related Maclachlan. "It would have been handy (for me) to commission on. But I want to be working with Ella for the next twenty years. I don't want her to turn around in two years and say, 'You took me for everything you could.'"

Not that Lorde and large amounts of money were strangers. It was a well-known fact that long before the singer signed on for the multi-million dollar publishing deal she had already made a considerable amount of money. That she had it and was not spotted buying big cars and houses was in stark contrast to the antics of other very young and very wealthy celebrities who seemed hell-bent on spending it faster than they made it.

Lorde would often get the money question and, as in the case of an interview with the *Today Show*, she was humble and straightforward in discussing it.

"All my money goes into a trust and I can't just take it

out spend it willy nilly," she said. "My dad has to okay it. I don't know if I would know how to live in a hugely extravagant way."

Songs head of A&R Ron Perry recalled in *Billboard* how the yearlong chase after Lorde began. "My A&R guy, Corey Roberts, picked up on her in January and sent me an email that said, 'Stop What You're Doing.' That was pretty ballsy considering he had only started working for us six weeks earlier. But I did. I flipped out right away."

Songs CEO Matt Pincus quickly fell in line and there began a persistent courtship of the soon-to-be seventeen year old. It seemed that a member of *Songs* had become a part of Lorde's touring company, with a representative being present at every live performance that year, getting to know Lorde and Machachlan and pointing out the advantages of signing with them. It did not hurt their chances that some of Lorde's favorite songwriters and producers, including The Weekend and Diplo were signed to Songs and she had, prior to the announcement, already been in informal talks about possible collaborations with several of Songs' clients.

It was around this time that Lorde casually acknowledged to *The Guardian* that she had been tinkering with collaborating for some time with others. And while she would not name names, she gave some insight into just how these collaborations had been working.

"Someone sends me a beat or they say they've got a hook and I'm doing all the verses. But I'm traveling so much at the moment there's no time to get in the room with anyone."

The Guardian conversation took place shortly after Lorde returned to New Zealand. She was about to appear at the Vodaphone Music Awards show and was relishing the idea of being home for a while. But she acknowledged that the traveling she had done in the past year, the places she had been and the people she had met had definitely influenced the way she now writes.

Speculation was now at fever pitch that when the Grammy nominations were announced on December 6, that Lorde would be represented in a number of categories. She was. The singer/songwriter received nomination nods for Song of the Year for "Royals," Record of the Year for "Royals," Best Pop Solo Performance for "Royals" and Best Pop Vocal Album for *Pure Heroine.*

Observers of the pop music scene were not surprised at the number of nominations Lorde received. Perhaps, more important, they were encouraged that, after a drought in which manufactured and vapid pop singers/teen idols were capturing the lions' share of the spotlight and far too many awards, the Grammy judges were suddenly getting behind a pop singer and songwriter of wit, intelligence and depth.

Lorde readily acknowledged her appreciation while deftly sidestepping the notion that she was galloping in on a figurative white horse to save popular music from its own worst tendencies.

Lorde had received an early Christmas present. She was now officially being recognized as a comer and a full-fledged star. How much better could it get for the seventeen year old remained to be seen.

CHAPTER FOURTEEN

UNDER PRESSURE

By early December, what was next became apparent when Lorde announced her 2014 North American tour. The fifteen-city tour, at least at this point, was conspicuous by the fact that there was no Los Angeles show scheduled and that much of the tour was settled in the Midwest and the East. The tour, scheduled to run March 3-26 included stops in Austin, Dallas, Houston, Washington D.C., Philadelphia, New York, Boston, Toronto, Detroit, Chicago, St. Louis, Kansas City, Denver, Seattle and Oakland.

Why she had chosen to pretty much ignore her early strongholds was brought into question by many tour journalists who speculated that a first tour would go to areas where her popularity was already established. However those who make their living by digging deeper may have wisely felt that an initial tour should break new ground. They also figured that token stops in places like New York and Los Angeles would 'magically' be added to the tour schedule.

Lorde had worked hard and, with the Grammys and her first full-blown US tour coming, she announced that she was taking a five-week break from performing and all but the most mandatory promotion. Pure and simple, Lorde needed a rest.

Many observers felt the break would also push back the

timetable on any new music. But as a Christmas gift to her fans, it was announced that an 'extended version' of *Pure Heroine*, which would include the original songs plus a generous six song sampling of songs from *The Love Club* EP, would be released.

Lorde was also active on the charity front during this time. When Typhoon Haiyan devastated the Philippines, causing untold death and destruction, a compilation charity album entitled *Songs for the Philippines,* was quickly assembled with all the proceeds targeted for Typhoon Haiyan relief efforts. The album, which featured songs by The Beatles, Bob Dylan, U2, Justin Timberlake and countless others, contained Lorde's "The Love Club."

While Lorde was quick to show her philanthropy for a worldwide cause, she had not forgotten her hometown roots. When the Devenport Community Garden Center had a shortfall in donations, Lorde and several other New Zealand notables painted a series of garden gnomes that would be auctioned off. Lorde was particularly happy that, in this small way, she could give back to the town that had meant so much to her.

Lorde also decided that it was time to begin weaning her fans off the early singles and surprised the world on December 13 when she released a tantalizing new single on iTunes.

"No Better," as befitting its creator, was slightly out of left field. The song was reportedly one of several that had been left off of *Pure Heroine* and, in announcing its release, Lorde stated that the song would not appear on another album. By now wise to the way of subtle promotion, Lorde's matter of fact approach to releasing "No Better" led to immediate response, untold number of downloads and, almost after the fact, another hit single.

More and more Lorde's impact on the US was being felt, even by such august publications as *Time*. The singer was named by the publication to its year end list, The 16 Most Influential Teens of 2013. The irony was that Lorde came in at No. 17 and thus missed the cut by one spot.

By mid-December, Lorde was reaping the benefits of the Grammy nominations. The downside was that her plate was full and getting fuller by the second. Unfortunately this meant that Lorde would have to cut back on commitments she had already made.

The first and to many, the most galling, was the announcement that she was backing out of an appearance at the Auckland Laneway Festival to concentrate on preparations for the upcoming Grammys. The promoters of the Laneway Festival issued a statement that they understood but, to many of her New Zealand fans, there was a grumbling that Lorde had suddenly gotten too big and was casting aside the audience who had been with her from the beginning.

The singer must have felt a bit of a backlash brewing and so quickly announced that she would perform a special hometown show at the festival site after the Grammy awards, in which those who had bought the original festival tickets would get in free. Lorde saved face in that instance but the consensus was that the continued pull of larger markets, especially America, would continue to force a juggling act.

Early into the New Year, Lorde was literally a star which was putting a real strain on an often and near manic desire for privacy. The expected adulation from her growing legion of fans was something she was grateful for and readily acknowledged.

But she had come to detest the intrusion of the paparazzi

and the tabloid press that had become a daily part of her life. It was midway through January, brought on by an incident in which Lorde and her family were nearly knocked down by swarming paparazzi, that Lorde would make her discomfort public with a series of tweets that were reported by numerous outlets including *The Huffington Post*.

"I'm beginning to get used to my image as a public commodity," she tweeted. "And the fact that I'm beginning to get used to it frightens me. There is a difference between the attention of fans, which I love, and the constant often lecherous gaze that I'm subjected to in this industry. I know that success comes with a price tag. It just sucks when you see that in your tiny home country where you previously felt safe."

Lorde would receive direct support for her battles with the press from former Crowded House member and New Zealand native Neil Finn who suggested in a conversation with *The Guardian* that Lorde might be better off leaving the country.

"Those news teams are idiots," he said. "New Zealand had been quite a good environment for her because people had not been super celebrity oriented and they pretty much leave you alone. But now it's reached critical mass. I think she might be better off moving to New York or someplace where there would be less bother about it."

Although Lorde continued to make New Zealand her home base, she did concede in a *Vanity Fair* interview that the increased attention has caused her to make some modifications in her everyday life. "I feel like I catch public transport slightly less than I did before. Which is kind of nice. But I still do take it quite a bit."

Not all the rumors and innuendo surrounding Lorde on her climb to the top were serious business. One of the more recurring was the notion that Lorde could not possibly be so talented and famous and really be only seventeen years old. Much gossip and Internet support for this theory fell on the fact that Lorde dressed and looked much older than her reported age.

While wildly absurd, this story hung around long enough for somebody to finally take steps to dispute it. That somebody was the website *The Hairpin* which performed due journalistic diligence by sending off for a copy of Lorde's birth certificate. Sure enough, the document indicated that Lorde was indeed seventeen. Even though the story quickly disappeared, the singer had no problem dredging it up upon meeting a *Vanity Fair* reporter in New York and having a good laugh at the idiocy of it all.

"Hi. I'm Ella and I'm actually forty-five," she laughed.

CHAPTER FIFTEEN
THE PROM ON 'ROIDS

Lorde may have been the biggest star on the planet. But until she left home to return to the States, she was still Ella. Which meant cleaning up her room before she left the house.

It was not long before Lorde was once again winging her way back to the States for a final round of preparation and promotion for her upcoming appearance at The Grammys. And rather than the white knuckle ride her first ever-long distance plane ride had been, this flight from New Zealand to Los Angeles was one big party. Lorde's entourage included her parents, siblings, her musical partner Joel Little and manager Maclahlan. The good spirits and cheer and all around excitement was palpable.

However for Lorde, It was also most likely a time of deep contemplation for the seventeen year old singer. In every sense of the word, she had arrived. She was established in a highly competitive pop music world. And the glory was that she had done it her way. Four Grammy nominations had been the icing on the cake. Grammy wins would be that extra emotional layer.

Like most teenagers, she was also having her doubts and insecurities. Many looked on the singer's success at such a young age as all good. But Lorde was only seventeen. Was this as good as it would get? Would it get better? Or would she finally turn out to be yet another short chapter and quickly flame out?

She was quick to tell *The Music* prior to her Grammy ride that she was already beginning to feel uneasy about the 'role model' tag that was being attached to her and that people should not be surprised when "I'm going to fuck some stuff up at some point because that's a natural part of becoming an adult."

In that same interview, Lorde would also take a revisionist look at her trademark song "Royals" and stated that it was not her best song. "I understand why it worked and why it was kind of a hit. But these melodies are not quite as good as something I would have written now and I definitely would not have written the lyric this way if I had written it now."

Lorde's family was enjoying the total Hollywood experience. To her way of thinking The Grammies was the end of a joyous year long ride as they experienced fame and fortune and celebrity right along with their daughter. Lorde's mother, Sonja, was both in awe and anxious in describing the days leading up to the actual ceremony in a conversation with radio station The Edge.

"We're relieved and proud. It was almost like a panic in the days leading up to the ceremony. Lorde's siblings have been blown away by it all."

Lorde tried real hard to be nonchalant about The Grammies and what awards might do to her already skyrocketing career but, in conversation with *The Hollywood Reporter*, all pretense of seriousness had gone out the window and she could barely contain the giggly child inside.

"It has been quite weird. I never saw myself as a Top 40

Princess. I do not want to get my hopes up in any way. But I would be pretty psyched to win a Grammy. I'm excited for everything that will go along with the day, seeing a bunch of my friends, dressing up, performing, will be really fun. It sounds like the prom on 'roids or something."

Lordes' plane touched down at LAX in Los Angeles the week of January 20. The singer was greeted at the airport by hundreds of fans, screaming, taking pictures and, for the few lucky ones, capturing a moment with their idol and an autograph. To those with a sense of history, it was Beatlemania revisited. For those with a sense of 'right now,' it was pure pop pandemonium.

The next few days flew by in a whirlwind of activity. There were the endless round of pre-Grammy interviews with a large run of gossipy questions about dates, her boyfriend, what she was going to be wearing on that special night and what she thought were her chances of walking off with a Grammy or four. By degrees Lorde seemed less about the music and more about having a good time, especially when she mixed and mingled with assorted peers and celebrities during a pre-Grammy party. But at the end of the day, Lorde was nothing if not in control.

Of particular note was the fact that Lorde had been selected to sing her song "Royals" live on stage during the many musical highlights of the show. Granted, her musicians and she had played "Royals" live so many times that there really was no need for anything beyond a sound check. But the reality was that The Grammys were very much about television and that it would most likely be that she would have to perform a somewhat truncated version of the song to accommodate awards presentations, commercials and that often intruding of time and keeping on schedule.

"I'm planning all of it," she said of her live performance to *Vanity Fair*. "Obviously I care about what I'm doing. We've done an alternative version of the music track and the visuals are really strong, simple and beautiful."

But as keyboard player MacDonald noted in a *New Zealand Musician* interview, the logistics of the show were not making it easy. "When we arrived for the sound check, we discovered that we would be playing on a stage in the middle of the arena and that there would be a delay coming out of the front house speakers. They also would not let us use our own monitor system. It made it pretty hard but we got there in the end."

When not in the pre-Grammy fishbowl, the singer was also hard at work, finalizing her makeup and wardrobe for that night. Lorde was not leaving anything to chance or to those assigned to help her who did not know her well enough to have a worthy opinion.

Through it all, the young woman managed to find a way to please the local fans who had been there for her but did not have the cachet of celebrity. On fairly short notice, Lorde pulled together a live performance at the hip and very compact Soho House. The performance, a mixture of her hits and some lesser heard songs, was a very informal present to the fans as well as a somewhat blatant pitch for everybody to watch the Grammys and put the singer at ease for her big night three days later.

But despite her best efforts, Lorde was most certainly a bundle of nerves and excitement as she and her musicians checked into the Staples Center for a sound check some hours before the show. From those on the scene as her limo dropped her off later that day, any nerves had effectively been masked by an air of excitement and a bright smile.

Although The Grammys would showcase a literal Who's Who of stars, Lorde's appearance was being touted as the one everybody was looking forward to. It was the performance that would be seen simultaneously by millions around the world.

Lorde knew this would be a big deal. What the audience did not know was that Lorde had a couple of visual surprises up her sleeve. She was well known for her long extremely curly hair and a propensity for dressing very Goth and all in black. The vision she presented as she walked out on the Grammy stage was of a fairly conservative, by Lorde standards, black and white pantsuit and long straight hair. But there was no mistaking that 'look' as she morphed out of the real world and into the depth and emotion of "Royals." There was a strength in her performance, a statement that only a true individual could make. Lorde smiled and thanked the audience before going off stage to thunderous applause.

The smile on her face said it all. Lorde was on cloud nine.

The only thing that could make the evening more memorable would happen later in the Grammy show when it was announced that the singer had captured Grammy awards for Best Record of the Year and Best Pop Solo Performance for the song "Royals."

In both instances Lorde gave appropriate and heart-felt speeches, thanked all the right people on her 'team' and thanked the countless fans for their support. But it would remain for this child of the Internet age to personally thank the millions when she tweeted sometime during the show. "I am so thankful for the attention my work has received tonight and this year."

If there was a warm and fuzzy element to the evening it was the fact that Lorde's parents were on hand to proudly watch their daughter take an all-important step in music and sharing all the glitz and glamor of the night. Victor and Sonja happily acknowledged that it was all very new and exciting to them to *Radio New Zealand*.

"As a mum, when I sat there, I was in shock. I was absolutely in shock."

Victor echoed his wife's sentiments. "You feel a bit dumbfounded when you hear your daughter's name called out amongst such company. We were both shocked but also thrilled."

In the excitement and celebration of the moment, Sonja matter-of-factly dropped a bombshell of sorts when she said that her daughter's Grammy victories had pretty much been her diploma for her chosen career. "Clearly she is not going to be going back to school," she reported. "Ella's chosen a career that stimulates her intelligence."

Lorde would be the center of attention at a number of post Grammy shindigs, gracefully accepting congratulations and wearing a constant ear to ear smile. The irony of how celebrity can trump reality amid the glitz and glamour of big time Hollywood was brought home during the round of parties when, after being on television and pictures of her seemingly everywhere, Lorde, despite her obvious youth, was let into a party without having to produce ID. She was a literal Cinderella at the ball and, much like Cinderella, the clock would strike midnight and it was time to return to the real world.

But not without one final private party for family and the closest of friends. After a night of hobnobbing with the rich and famous at the after show parties, Lorde and her family returned to their hotel. It was 3:00 a.m. But as Sonja recalled in conversation with The Edge, the party was not quite over.

In a spontaneous moment of joy and celebration, Lorde and her family jumped into the hotel pool with all their clothes on.

"It was goodbye suit. Goodbye Grammy frock. We were all dripping wet and surrounded by people we knew and liked and wanted to be around."

Lorde awoke fairly early the next morning and went shopping in Hollywood with some friends. Later that day she was back on board a big jetliner and taxiing down the runway into a bright sky. Emotionally Lorde was on top of the world.

Now she was going home.

Lorde's Grammy wins had an immediate impact on her Internet status. According to a *New York Times* article, an estimated 200,000 twitter friends were added to Lorde's friends' status within twenty-four hours of her winning the Grammys. It was also reported that ticket sales for Lorde's January 29 show in Auckland had jumped on news of her Grammy wins.

Lorde's plane touched down at Auckland Airport the morning of January 29. The singer and her entourage had just entered the international arrivals area when a deafening roar went up. Hundreds of fans had staked out the airport and were cheering their conquering hero. After the initial shock and surprise, Lorde was quite happy to wade into the crowd and take pictures with her fans and sign autographs. She also talked briefly to the assembled press.

But her welcome home was not without its rough moments. The swarming New Zealand media were particularly aggressive in trying to photograph the singer and one could see from the look on her face that she was not comfortable with this pushy press intrusion on her moment of good cheer. She tweeted as much not long after her return to New Zealand.

"I understand that people of note are supposedly fair game for everyone to photograph and film. But that doesn't make it acceptable. New Zealand media almost pushed my family and myself over in order to get their shots. A bit of a sad welcome if I'm honest."

But Lorde would remain remarkably cordial in patently answering the interviewer's obvious, softball questions.

She insisted in a story that appeared in *The Daily Life* that winning the previous years' New Zealand Music Awards had been more intense than the Grammys. "I feel like I was more freaking when I won my New Zealand awards to be honest," she said. "It's super cool (the Grammys) but it becomes a normal thing once you're amongst it."

Likewise, Joel expressed to *The Daily Life* a sincere sense of disbelief at the Grammy triumphs and his feelings about being home. "This is the highlight for all of us, being back in New Zealand. It was great being in L.A. but coming back to this and the well-wishers, I'm really chuffed and I know Lorde is too."

Lorde continued to be accommodating with her fans, right up until the point when she was gently prodded by her handlers toward the exit, followed by a crowd of screaming, supportive fans who had gotten the autograph, the photo, perhaps the quick word.

Lorde finally made her way through the airport and disappeared into the day. In a perfect world, she would be heading home to relax. But Lorde would, instead, be back on stage that night in front of thousands of adoring fans.

For Lorde, this was the perfect world.

And for her mother it was a time to hold back tears as the notion of mother and daughter was now forever linked to celebrity. "I'm never letting her go," Sonja told *The Edge.*

"That's where you become unstuck with your kids. You don't ever let them go but you let them move out a little bit.

"You guide them along their path."

CHAPTER SIXTEEN

SILLY SEASON

The Laneway Festival that night was an ideal homecoming and a way to say thank you to Lorde's home country.

Admittedly still jet-lagged and still riding high on the wave of emotion from her Grammy wins, Lorde reportedly put on a complete and polished performance. Some of the British press, in a more nattering than vicious way, pointed out that the show was indicative of how Lorde's act could become a bit tedious, despite the strength of her songs and her haunting stage presence, because of the minimalist nature of the music. But fans don't usually listen to what critics say and so, for those at the show, the experience was first rate.

Although continuously loyal to places like New Zealand and Australia, behind the scenes, pressure continued to build that would ultimately tear Lorde away from her base of support. Lorde's brand of musical creativity was suddenly riding the crest of huge pop music business. Suddenly bands and performers with an edgier, less obvious approach were being sought out and signed. No one could deny that the success of Lorde had brought about a much hoped for renaissance.

But by February, it appeared that big business, as it pertained to Lorde, might just be winning out.

Lorde took a few days off for some rest and relaxation in

Paris. The City of Lights was very much her emotional layover. She walked the streets, experienced the art and culture and, along with boyfriend James, felt the vibe of easy living that, momentarily took her away from her professional world.

Lorde was very much the young woman while in Paris, resorting to a midnight selfie picture of herself without makeup and spots of acne cream on her face. The shot would immediately go viral. It was good, harmless fun that, to Lorde's way of thinking, pointed up the fact that she was not flawless or fake and that, at the end of the day, she was just like everybody else.

But like everything else in Lorde's world, the notion that she might be a normal teenage girl who had occasional breakouts of acne was turned into a major news story by those gossip columnists who made their living off the insignificant crumbs of celebrities' lives.

Shortly after the Paris trip, it was announced that, despite the upcoming US tour, Lorde would also be making an appearance at this year's Coachella Festival in California and that, come May, she would be the special musical attraction at the legendary Preakness Horse Race Infield Fest in Baltimore It was plain from these announcements that those making the business decisions for Lorde were going all out in the US market. Which ultimately resulted in another announcement that Lorde had cancelled an upcoming Australian tour.

There was some grumbling that Lorde had suddenly gotten too big for her leggings. But at the end of the day, success in popular music was, at its core, a numbers game and the numbers in Australia were dwarfed by the possibilities in America.

Possibilities that had been borne out by the fact that Lorde's upcoming US tour had sold out in a matter of days.

Lorde excitedly tweeted the news to her fans. "You sold out my US tour!"

The news immediately set management and concert promoters into overdrive as they attempted to add further dates to the tour. This was not proving too difficult a task as witness the fact that her New York show quickly spawned a second date.

One element of Lorde's life quickly changed. Despite being well into her final year of secondary schooling, the idea that Lorde would suddenly drop everything so she could take finals and graduate with her classmates was now dim. Her mother had already said as much during her *Radio New Zealand* conversation. Lorde would be less sure on the issue in a question and answer session with Reditt. "I'm really not sure yet. Obviously it would be hard to do at the moment."

With the Grammy fervor slowly disappearing and no new news of substance in the days leading up to the start of the US tour, there was a bit of a dry spell for Lorde gossip, which inevitably led to a bit of the 'silly season' as totally outlandish items began to appear that had no basis in reality.

There was the old chestnut "Lorde is dead." It was also time for the not unexpected "Lorde has secretly married" or was pregnant or had broken up with James stories to appear and just as quickly disappear.

Not every Lorde story would turn out to be false. When the singer's dog, Spinee, was suddenly taken ill and required immediate and risky surgery, Lorde was all over the Internet asking her legions of fans to pray for her dog's recovery. She would update the world on her dog's progress for the next twenty-four hours and then happily reported that Spinee was on the mend.

A much more sinister story broke in February when it was

reported that nude photos allegedly taken by Lorde during her recent trip to Paris were now all over the internet and had been published by at least one celebrity magazine. Authorities were immediately on the case, as were Lorde's legal team. Sadly Lorde had learned a valuable lesson about privacy and the fact that she was a celebrity meant she had very little of it.

Lorde's representatives were becoming a bit more unresponsive when it came to stories about their charge, which only gave credence to stories that would surface regarding her future plans. The latest being that the singer had a security guard posted in front of Golden Age Studios where Lorde had as many as eight new songs in various stages of development. As an aside, the same reports indicated that Lorde was planning a world tour towards the end of 2015.

The young singer was amused at the speculation surrounding any new music but she couched her amusement in introspection in conversation with The New Zealand Listener. "Oh that pressure. I don't feel it. I feel like whatever I make is going to be so much better than what I've made. Of course it's all well and good to say that when the second album is not even out yet."

The reality was that Lorde, during February, was moderately busy on the performing and promotion front. Reportedly in the wake of her cancelling her Australia tour, Lorde attempted to mend some fences with a quick promotion trip to Sydney where, during an interview with radio station Triple J, she confessed that her sudden level of celebrity was anything but normal.

"What I'm going through is so abnormal," she remarked during the radio interview that was reported by *Radio.com*. "I feel like a lot of people of my level don't write about it because a lot of what we do is so boring. It's interesting for me to write about the weird little details of doing what I do."

During the interview Lorde unveiled a new song in her list, a cover of James Blake's song "Retrograde', which had its official debut in Lorde's hands during her January appearance in the Laneway Festival. As it would turn out, Lorde would not be the only one unveiling covers to the masses. In February, Lorde's younger sister, India, made a minor Internet splash when she covered the song "Say Something" by the group A Great Big World.

As another olive branch toward soothing hurt feelings in Australia, Lorde performed at the country's annual ARPA awards show. If the spontaneous and lasting applause was any indication, any alleged slights between Lorde and the Aussies had been forgotten.

Lorde's rapidly rising star was also beginning to carry over to other parts of the world. In the wake of her Grammy and New Zealand awards triumph, it was announced that the singer had been nominated for Best International Solo Artist by the prestigious Brit Awards whose ceremony was slated for February 19 at the London 02 Arena. Adding a bit of excitement to what could most certainly be a by-the-numbers awards appearance was the rumor that Lorde and the up and coming British white noise group Disclosure might well do an on stage collaboration of her song "Royals." As it would turn out the rumor was fact and, in a conversation with radio station Capital FM, she was enthusiastic about stretching her wings in a truly collaborative state

"The Brits were like 'Would you be open to this?' and I was like 'Yes this is so my thing.' I think it's going to be pretty special. I'm really proud of it. They're (the group) are super easy to work with and so it's been fun."

And that fun would translate into a major music mash-up on the night of the awards show as Lorde sang "Royals" aided and abetted by Disclosure's sonic contributions. The evening was made complete when Lorde walked off with Best International Female Solo Artist. Lorde acknowledged in a post awards press conference that she was "overwhelmed" by winning the award. "You simply don't expect to win awards when you're up against people like Gaga, Pink and others."

While on the surface Lorde continued to move through this brave new world of sudden pop stardom with relative ease, there were indications that the constant scrutiny and exposure were beginning to be overwhelming. More and more she was appreciating the time away from the spotlight and the opportunity to be with her family and friends and to just be Ella rather than Lorde, an alter ego that was suddenly seemingly everywhere. Which inevitably led to the tags of Lorde as some kind of role model. She would address that issue in a *Vogue Magazine* conversation.

"There's a fine line between role model and preaching to people," she said. "I never want to tell anyone how they should be, especially not someone my age. But I'm conscious of the fact that people my age are reading what I say and listening to what I say. And that's cool, especially for the girls who are into what I do."

Lorde's tone of even-handedness when it came to the role model question came as a bit of a surprise. But to her logical way of thinking, in certain quarters, she was exactly that. For better or worse.

There was a particular tone of fatigue and no small amount of resignation in a recent interview with *V Magazine*.

She acknowledged that the sentiments represented in the lyrics of "Royals" do not reflect the place that sudden celebrity has thrust her into. She also seemed mentally up to here with hearing her music everywhere she turned and assumed that even her loyal fans might be feeling the same way.

"I want to let people stop hearing Lorde on the radio all the time because it's kind of crazy at the moment," she told *V*. "I'd like to give people a little bit of breathing room before I unleash something different."

She quietly bristled at the *V* interviewer's notion that she was being tagged with the dreaded 'voice of a generation' label after barely a year. That was the last thing she wanted to hear.

"If people start hearing that about me, they're going to say 'Fuck off!'"

CHAPTER SEVENTEEN

SURPRISE

In the days and weeks leading up to Lorde's first US tour, there would be a lot of speculation and one or two surprises.

Preparations for the upcoming US tour began in earnest. It was a given that Lorde would now be performing a much longer set and so the singer and her band were settled with working some additional tunes into the show's song list. There were also some tweaks to the presentation of the music as well as the stage set up to consider.

Apparently Lorde's attention to stage details has been in preparation for a while as was acknowledged during an interview with *Rookie Magazine*. "I've been writing for what I want to happen onstage for the tour as well as the next music video. I also have been working on some ideas for some kind of television program."

But while she was seemingly on an endless ride of being pulled in every conceivable direction at once, Lorde was amazingly calm and about the work even in what many would consider an ongoing, hellish schedule. The singer would admit that what she was going through was the fun part of the deal in conversation with radio station Live 105.

"I like it. I'm having fun. I make sure that I'm not overwhelmed with stuff to do every day so I actually look forward to it. No, I don't feel much pressure. I think I felt pressure writing the first record. But because I had success with one of my first songs, it all became normal to me very quickly."

Lorde would spend long- hours fine-tuning the specifics of the tour. Although she had become quite familiar on US shores, she was taking great pains to make her first official American tour something special and something done her way.

Which meant the possibility of mixing in some as yet new and unreleased songs. Her cover of Tears for Fears' "Everybody Wants to Rule the World" was a possibility as was her take on the James Blake song "Retrograde." And she had already seen the impact her version of Kanye West's "Hold My Liquor" could have on an audience.

In an interview with *Rookie*, Lorde tantalizingly offered up a very brief listen to a song in the works called "Hospitals." She was mum on where or when the song might appear. These kinds of hints quickly had the Internet abuzz with speculation about how the next batch of Lorde songs would sound. At this point the singer was not offering a whole lot of particulars. But she did indicate in conversation with *Rookie* that there was some experimentation afoot.

"I've been playing around with all instrumental tracks and have laid down some long blues jams," she offered.

Apparently it's been a lot more than playing around. In a recent *Billboard* interview, the singer nonchalantly disclosed that she had been finding time between all the touring, promotion and Grammy hoopla to actually get some serious songwriting done. "I have been writing but I haven't really had the time to hit the studio and get some things down on tape. That will be sometime next year."

Lorde's level of notoriety had by this time reached a point where even the more mainstream media was willing to take a flyer on the New Zealand singer. A case in point being CNN International who pieced together a warm and fuzzy, but no less interesting, piece on Lorde's pre-stardom days in school that featured memories from teachers, principals and classmates. It was a piece that brought home the point with no amount of subtlety that Lorde was quite literally an overnight success.

Easily the most shocking announcement in a while came when Lorde announced that Taylor Swift and she were seriously thinking about doing some music together. It was an announcement that caught everybody by surprise and immediately divided musical camps.

You'd have to search long and hard to find two people who were from such different places musically. Some observers speculated that it was the wrong thing to do and might result in a flood of less intellectually inclined teen stars beating down her door for some street cred. Still others felt that this 'slumming' with inferior but commercially successful acts could increase Lorde's mainstream appeal. That Lorde and Swift had suddenly become the best of friends was documented in February when the singer, in Los Angeles, was spotted out going to the beach and shopping with Swift.

In a Capital FM conversation, Lorde made a spirited defense that such an oil and water collaboration could work. "Yeah, we are different. But I think the cool thing about Taylor is she is willing to go a lot of places with music. I think her last record in particular (Red), everyone was like 'Whoa! A lot of ground has been covered.' And I think that with an artist like her, the sky is the limit."

The possibility of a Taylor Swift collaboration almost immediately made it open season for any journalist stuck for a news item to pop the 'who would you like to work with' question and depending on her mood that day, Lorde's responsive would either be humorous or serious speculation. The interviewer at *Clash* struck pay dirt with that question.

"Rihanna would be fun to write for because she's done everything. And I'd also like to write for or with Ellie Goulding. Girl bands are only cool if they're ridiculous. I'd write for a Korean girl band. Some of their melodies are the best pop."

Lorde was not the only one savoring this rocket to stardom. Her drummer Ben Barter acknowledged in *Modern Drummer* that the past year had been an amazing one for him. "It's been the fastest and most exciting year of my life. I've managed to tick many of my musical aspirations off."

He also explained how touring with Lorde had given him firsthand insights into how age was not a factor when it came to creativity. "Touring this past year has been such a blast. Ella is amazing to work with. I feel fortunate to play for an artist whose music I love and respect."

Barter would not be the only one to benefit from Lorde's massive success. Joel was also reaping the rewards for being tied so closely to "Royals." In the wake of Lorde's success, he began working with a New Zealand duo called Broods, began writing with Silverchair's David Johns on his solo album and was tied, in various writing and production capacities to Sam Smith, Kwabs and Jetta.

"It's definitely opened up some doors," he understatedly told *Billboard*. "Having a hit single makes people take a bit more notice."

Lorde had been notoriously stingy when it came to licensing her music. But the rare item that struck her fancy came along midway through February when she agreed to let a mash-up of her song "Glory and Gore" appear over a trailer for a second season preview of the History Channel's series *Vikings*. But she acknowledged in a personal look back on her career in *Sunday Magazine* that she was not inclined to just give away her songs to anything just for the bucks. "If I granted every sandwich place, skincare product and coming of age blockbuster use of my songs I would be a millionaire. But I'm extremely fussy."

It was around this time that Lorde took a busman's holiday and, for reportedly the first time, worked on somebody else's music, in this case the song "Easy" (Switching Screens) by alternative musician and producer Son Lux. The song in question was a dark outing with horror film overtones, the ideal venue for Lorde to lay down some intricate and subtle vocals. Working with somebody whose music she admired was the kind of creative exercise she craved and it wet her appetite for other such side projects in the future.

Reports began filtering back to New Zealand about the frenzy being generated in anticipation of the upcoming US tour that would most certainly break her out on a grand scale. But in interviews given post-Grammy, it had become evident that the singer had matured into a special place where she had happily acknowledged her success but was keeping it all low key and philosophical rather than jumping up and down and manic. It was a state of grace, that she offered in *Rolling Stone*.

"I have to keep reminding myself that this is my life."

CHAPTER EIGHTEEN

ART . . . WHAT IT IS

A date in Phoenix, Arizona was just added. That the Phoenix show was scheduled for April 17, a good three weeks after the last reported date of the tour made it obvious that Lorde would not be finishing what had been projected as a relatively short tour anytime soon.

In fact those in the know speculated that the whole idea of a limited tour had always had a back door to adding more shows once the tour became 'a must see' event. It was further being tossed around that once the dust settled, Lorde might not truly finish her first US tour until sometime in June.

Lorde knew she was packing for a long haul. She just was not sure how long the haul would be. A second show was added in Oakland, followed by a quick jump to South America for shows in Chile, Brazil and Argentina. Then back to the states for shows in Indio for the first of two Coachella appearances, Las Vegas, and a second show in Indio. This would take the singer through to the end of April. But the phones were ringing all over the world so it was a safe bet that Lorde would be on the road for a good portion of 2014.

Lorde and the band were well-rehearsed. The consensus was that a longer show would be a better show and more clearly define the creative force that, in the course of only a year, had turned her into a truly special kind of performer. Lorde and her people were still attempting to keep the presentation simple. But it was expected that her entourage would be bigger and that the demands on her time would be greater.

There were most likely people looking out for Lorde's day-to-day wellbeing in the days leading up to the start of the tour. Signs of excitement and pre-tour nerves were to be expected. Lorde had not completely gotten over those.

Lorde was seventeen. A normal seventeen year old who was suddenly not so normal. She had doubts, insecurities and, yes, fears. But, as she explained in an intimate look at her rise to the top in *Sunday Magazine*, she had met her demons head on and was dealing with them.

"Sometimes I feel so lonely, I don't want to do it anymore. But truth is, I love what I do so much. I've never been so happy or worked so hard. Adults like to ask me how I'm coping with things, because adults are always nervous that there's a looming breakdown on the horizon. But what I say is that for all the moments that I dislike, there are these moments where everything is slow motion, full color, sweet."

The singer remains alternately heartened and amazed by the fact that her career has happened so fast. As she explained in *3rd Degree*, the mere notion of having a music career, let alone one at such a young age, was pure fantasy.

"It feels like the most natural thing in the world to me because I've never had anyone else's music career. I get to do these crazy things that a lot of other people wouldn't necessarily get to do."

Lorde did her best to make the rounds of longtime friends, spending time with her family and finding time just for herself. She would often most likely be found in quiet contemplation, looking at the world with pencil and paper in hand, fashioning lyrics, looking to the future.

She would acknowledge that the coming year would bring a lot more. New music, lots of performances and, most importantly a reinforcement of self. And so as the day finally arrived when she sat in a plane as it taxied down an Auckland Airport runway and into the sky, Lorde was ultimately at peace with her past, present and, most certainly, her future. A future she brought full circle in her looking inward in *Sunday Magazine*.

"I'm an artist, an author with a hunger for showing people what I can do and a talent for making people turn my name into a call while they're waiting front row.

"It's me. I'm here."

MARCH MADNESS

But before she could get there, Lorde was continuing to make waves in one form or another. She awoke on the morning of March 1 to the news that *Pure Heroine* had officially sold one million copies in the United States. Her already worldwide credibility received an even bigger boost on March 2 when it was reported by New Musical Express that Bruce Springsteen did a cover of "Royals" during his concert in Auckland.

Lorde was visibly moved when she heard of Springsteen's acoustic cover that opened his show, responding in tweets as reported by *News.com.au.* "My twitter went mental. Everyone in New Zealand was like 'you can't believe what just happened.' It was so exciting. It was the highest honor. I got a little teary. It was very cool."

And, as she would explain to *Starpulse,* it would also bring into perspective how quickly a song can ride the trail from obscure to classic. "It's crazy when someone like that is covering your song. Those words were nothing before I put them into my laptop and started messing around with them in the studio. It's crazy to me that they could come out of somebody else's mouth who is that respected."

Predictably the call for Lorde live was growing daily. Following the conclusion of the US dates, the singer was

scheduled to go to Brazil and Chile to appear in those coun-
tries' Lolapalooza Festivals before returning to the States in
April for her appearance at Coachella. And although no new
dates had been announced past April 18, more than one media
outlet was stating that the US tour would now go until May 17.

Any thoughts of Lorde getting homesick for James were
immediately dashed when the love of her life reported in a
story by the *New Zealand Herald* that he would be travelling
with his girlfriend throughout the tour.

What those who had planned the tour had not counted on
was the weather. For some weeks prior to the start of the tour,
a good part of the Midwest, South and East had been experiencing the worst cold snap in recent history. Rain, snow, icy
roads, funnel clouds and blizzard like sub- zero weather had
been battering much of the country and as Lorde settled into
the beginning of the tour, there was no sign of the bad weather
letting up.

First stop Austin, Texas. On the surface Austin seemed
a rather daring choice to begin a tour. Texas in general had a
rather conservative musical lineage, more rough and tumble
and basic emotions, not necessarily a state that would embrace
deep thoughts. However in recent years, Austin had become a
mecca for those who danced on the edge and a growing audience for music that defied preconceived notions. And nobody
could argue with the fact that the show had sold out in record
time.

However the singer was not leaving anything to chance.
She reportedly arrived in Austin two days before her scheduled concert and immediately set to work rehearsing every
element of her performance, an estimated six hours according
to hall observers, well into the night. At one point her fans

received a tweet, updating her preparations. "I forgot about the Oscars and just kept the crew til midnight. Getting the show perfect. See you tomorrow Austin."

When pressed by ABC News about what fans could expect at her show, Lorde offered, "It will be very simple. Cool lights. Just me being Gollum on stage and mucking around."

The anticipation of opening night quickly became a cause for celebration as Lorde moved silently and alone out of the stage blackness and, literally and figuratively alone, launched into 'Glory And Gore.' Shortly after, a curtain parted to reveal her band who, with the aid of some pre -recorded musical tracks, provided a dark and hard backbone for Lorde's vocals to freely roam. All the by now trademark lyrical, vocal and stage flourishes were on display in a seventy-minute set that showcased the singer as the master of her domain; offering up an enticing array of inflections, emotional shifts and haunting pop interpretation that gave even the familiarity of most of the set a new patina of power and depth.

And Lorde was nothing if not liberal in her song selection. Yes, all the hits and the favored tracks were on display. But the singer also showed that she could by playful with the inclusion of two strategically placed covers, "Swingin' Party," her Replacements homage and a heretofore unheard, at least in a live setting, "Easy" (Switching Screens) by Son Lux. Lorde could do no wrong on opening night and, if this were any indication, the rest of the tour would be aces.

Lorde pulled into Houston in high spirits. The reviews of the Austin show had been uniformly excellent. Given the precision required, the band and the technical elements were spot on. For one night at least, Lorde had truly conquered.

The following night in Dallas, the show took on even more

of a celebratory tone as the audience was alternately enraptured and joyous as they watched Lorde move through her distinctive array of songs with confidence and ease. While the majority of reviews of the Dallas show were near rapturous in their praise, some skeptics were not quite on board, sighting the continued brevity of her set, the minimalist music backing that sometimes slipped over into sameness and the bottom line damning with faint praise of Lorde of an artist who was destined for greater things but, in their eyes, was not quite there yet.

But she would prove at the Houston gig that it would only get better. Houston fans were seeing her for the first time and they were seeing a lot according to reviewers and rabid texters. Her unorthodox stage presence proved an enticing adjunct to her songs, adding a sense of tension and drama, even to songs that fans were by now overly familiar with. With two shows under her belt, her voice was now even more of a towering presence. And rather than a three ring circus of lights and pyrotechniques, the show's reliance on muted shades of dark and shadow proved a haunting but appropriate set piece to the overall tone of the show.

Early on in the tour, critics seemed captivated by the ease in which the singer was able to reimagine her songs to a more captivating and exploratory live setting. Reportedly the singer was so intent on getting things different and right on a daily basis that she and her band were rehearsing an average of six hours a day before each show.

But while the performances were rapidly falling in line as first rate. Mainstream press was beginning to notice and, as was their want, taking a deeper questioning look at her as a cultural icon and pop phenomena. *The Wall Street Journal*, in particular laid out a solid, even handed account, big on sales figures and other elements that landed firmly on the economic side. The story was also quick to point out that Lorde had made her impact in the US on the wings of one album and a couple of hit singles and openly questioning whether so much so soon was enough to define a career.

That line of speculation was nothing new for Lorde to ponder. *The Love Club* EP had barely been released when she was already contemplating the notion of being yet another flash in the pop music pan. Realistically she realized that her seeming core teen audience had notoriously short attention spans and that it was a real possibility that she might lose her audience and be another classic 'burn out' by age twenty one.

Lorde would continue speculating on her newness and the possibility of it all suddenly disappearing in *The Wall Street Journal*. "I'm green enough that I'm afraid that I'll wake up one day and it'll be gone. I still ask myself is my life interesting enough to write about?"

For now the answer seemed an emphatic yes.

The tour moved on to Washington D.C. with a performance that indicated there would be subtle changes and shifts within a fairly tightly formatted show. Predictably Lorde's emotional range carried the day, exploring the worlds of drive and ambition in a taut, believable manner. But the proceedings were lightened up considerably with several calls to the audience to sing a long during the course of the fourteen song set. And the show was predictably layered and dense, a good thing in Lorde's world as the singer gave free reign to explore seemingly endless emotional highs and lows.

It would become evident as the tour continued that Lorde was quite capable of keeping things interesting and that those on the back end of the tour would, most certainly, receive their own level of surprises amid the music that had brought them to pop music prayer.

The shows and the rave reviews continued to reinforce the fact that Lorde, in little more than a year, had truly arrived as a sanctified pop intellect, assured of herself as an artist, confident in her talent and its ability to grow and her future as that rare performer whose pure intellect will be the driving force. Lorde has always made it known that she was raised a by product of a different age, a universe that runs to technology while, at the same time, holding a reverent place in its soul for people who dare to be different, who dare to be smart.

Lorde's life and career are in play on an ever-evolving stage. She is an international kid who, while still some months shy of coming to majority as an adult, moves among the creative people and their adoring fans. It's a world she often reflects on and in a way that only Lorde can.

"If you see me and I'm whispering to myself, and seeming all crazy, don't worry," she said to *The New Zealand Listener*. It's just a happy mantra of thanks for the way things are."

DISCOGRAPHY

ALBUMS

PURE HEROINE (2013)
SONGS: "Tennis Court," 400 Lux," "Royals," "Ribs," "Buzz-cut Season," "Team," "Glory and Gore," "Still Sane," White Teeth Teens," "A World Alone."

PURE HEROINE, EXTENDED VERSION (2013)
SONGS: "Tennis Court," "400 Lux," "Royals," "Ribs," "Buzz-cut Season," "Team," "Glory and Gore," "Still Sane," "White Teeth Teens," "A World Alone," "No Better," "Bravado," "Million Dollar Bills," "The Love Club," "Biting Down," "Swingin' Party."

EPS

THE LOVE CLUB (2013)
SONGS: "Bravado," "Royals," "Million Dollar Bills," "The Love Club," "Biting Down."

TENNIS COURT (2013)
SONGS: "Tennis Court," "Swingin' Party," "Biting Down," "Bravado."

LIVE IN CONCERT (2013)
SONGS: "Buzzcut Season," Swingin' Party," "400 Lux," "Royals."

COMPILATION ALBUMS

SONGS FOR THE PHILLIPINES (2013)
The song "The Love Club."

SINGLES

"ROYALS," Released March 19, 2013.

"TENNIS COURT," Released Jun7, 2013.

"TEAM," Released September 13, 2013.

"NO BETTER," Released December 13, 2013.

SOUNDTRACKS

HUNGER GAMES: CATCHING FIRE (2013)
Lorde sings the Tears for Fears song "Everybody Wants to Rule the World"

PROMOTIONAL SINGLES

TOP CHART POSITIONS
"BRAVADO" – US # 29
"BUZZCUT SEASON" – US #29"RIBS" – US # 26
OTHER CHARTED SONGS
"THE LOVE CLUB" – New Zealand # 17. US #18
"SWINGIN' PARTY" – New Zealand #10
"MILLION DOLLAR BILLS" – US #29
"400 LUX" – US #20
"GLORY AND GORE" – US #20
"WHITE TEETH TEENS" – US #33
"A WORLD ALONE" – US #38
"STILL SANE" – US # 39
"EVERYBODY WANTS TO RULE THE WORLD" – New Zealand # 14. US # 30

AWARDS AND NOMINATIONS

Lorde received numerous nominations and awards during her year at the top of the charts. What follows are the confirmed awards and nominations from throughout the world. At the time of this publication, several other awards and nominations were pending.

APRA
Lorde won *The Silver Scroll Award* for the song "Royals"

BRIT AWARDS
Lorde won top honors for *International Female Solo Artist.*

GRAMMY AWARDS
Lorde won awards for *Song of the Year* and *Best Pop Solo Performance* for "Royals." The singer was nominated for *Record of the Year* for "Royals" and for *Best Pop Vocal Album* for *Pure Heroine.*

MTV EUROPE MUSIC AWARDS
Lorde captured top honors for *Best New Zealand Act* and was nominated for *Artist on the Rise.*

MTVU PEOPLE OF THE YEAR
Lorde won the award for *Woman of the Year.*

NEW ZEALAND MUSIC AWARDS
The singer won *Single of the Year* for "Royals," *Breakthrough Artist of the Year* for *The Love Club* EP, the *People's Choice Award* and the *International Achievement Award.*

NEW MUSICAL EXPRESS AWARDS
Lorde was nominated for *Best Solo Artist.*

PEOPLE'S CHOICE AWARDS
The singer was nominated for *Favorite Breakout Artist.*

A LITTLE ABOUT JOEL

Most observers of Lorde's rise to stardom just assume that her producer/co-writer Joel Little sprang magically into her life. But Joel, also a New Zealander born and raised, had an extensive career on the New Zealand scene well before Lorde stepped into his life.

Joel made his first big splash on the local music scene in 2001 when he was part of the hugely popular local band Goodnight Nurse. Joel sang and played guitar in this pop/punk hybrid outfit between its formation in 2001 and its 'indefinite hiatus in 2010." During this period Goodnight Nurse was a fixture on the New Zealand touring circuit.

Joel quite naturally grew into the songwriting role for the group. Many of the songs written for Goodnight Nurse's two albums, *Always and Never* (2006) and *Keep Me on Your Side* (2008) were written, co-written and produced by Joel. These included the singles "Loner," "Taking Over," "Going Away," "Our Song," "Death Goes to Disco," "All of You," "The Night," "I Need This," "This Is It" and "Lady with Me."

Following the disbanding of Goodnight Nurse, Joel took over the production and much of the writing chores on former Goodnight Nurse musician Sam McCarthy's spinoff electro pop group Kids at 88. This venture proved extremely creative for Joel and produced two albums, *Sugarpills* in 2010 and *Modern Love* in 2012 and a trio of chart singles, "My House," "Just A Little Bit" and "Downtown."

Joel also took a songwriting and production flyer with Australian reality show star turned pop star for the song "AYO That's What I Like" for the album *Timomatic*. Post Lorde he is also heavily involved in producing and writing an EP entitled *Broods* by a pop duo of the same name.

And further down the road? Well, Joel can expect a call from Lorde anytime now. Because the pair still have a lot of work to do.

SOURCES

Lorde: Your Heroine owes a lot to the dedicated journalists who would discover everything there was to know about the singer and Lorde's willingness, once she decided to do press, to talk to literally everybody and about everything. Thanks to the true media professionals and to Lorde for willingly letting people into her world.

MAGAZINES
Billboard, Rolling Stone, Metro, New Zealand Listener, Spin, Forbes, New York Magazine, Macleans', New Musical Express, The Australian, US, Vanity Fair, Vogue, V Magazine, Modern Drummer, New Zealand Musician, Clash.

NEWSPAPERS
The Telegraph, The Sydney Morning Herald, Sunday Magazine, The Guardian, The Daily Telegraph, The Devenport Flagstaff, The North Shore Times, The New Zealand Herald, The Nelson Mail, The San Jose Mercury News, The Associated Press, The Dominion Post, The Hollywood Reporter, The New York Times, The Arizona Daily Star, The Sun, The Village Voice, The Wall Street Journal, The Observer, Herald on Sunday, Chicago Sun Times.

WEBSITES
Pollstar.com, Spotify.com, Faster/Louder.com, Rookie.com, Stereogum.com, HitQuarters.com, www.new.com.au, Red Bull Music. com, Vulture.com, Stuff.com, Allmusic.com, Bullett.com, Grantland. com, The Vine.com, The Huffington Post.com, GQ.Qblog, The Music. com, Discus.com, The Cut.com, James Lowe's website, Daily Entertainment News.com, Fader.com, The Music Network.com, The Daily Life.com, Reditt.com, Radio.com, PopCrush.com, The World According To Lorde, Feministing, Clik Music.com, Teen Vogue.com.

RADIO

News Talk ZB, MTV, Triple J, Capital FM, 95.5 WPLJ, Radio New Zealand, KROQ, KCRW, ABC News, 97.1AMP, The Edge, Live 105.

TELEVISION

CNN International, 3rd Degree, VH-1, 3 News, The Today Show, Skavlan.

SOMEONE LIKE ADELE (UPDATED EDITION)

By Caroline Sanderson

Read the full, enthralling story of the 20-something London girl who took the music world by storm.

This fully updated paperback edition of the bestselling biography, **Someone Like Adele**, also now includes the story of how Adele found happiness with boyfriend (and rumoured husband) Simon Konecki; became a mother; and came to record the towering theme song for the James Bond movie, *Skyfall*.

Find out about her upbringing as the child of a single mother in north London and her time at the BRIT School for Performing Arts & Technology in Croydon where her peers included Leona Lewis and Jessie J.

Learn how her early performances after graduating from the BRIT school along with a MySpace demo led to her being signed up XL Records, and then voted the Brit Awards Critics' Choice even before her debut album, 19, was released.

Discover how real-life heartbreak inspired many of her iconic songs, including 'Rolling in the Deep' and 'Someone Like You'; and how a diverse range of musical influences - from the Spice Girls and Gabrielle to Etta James and contemporary Nashville sounds - contributed to her record-smashing second album, 21.

Available from www.omnibuspress.com

ISBN: 978.1.78038.863.2
Order No: OP55121

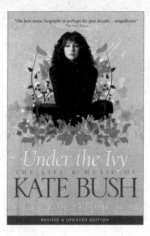

UNDER THE IVY: THE LIFE & MUSIC OF
KATE BUSH

By Graeme Thomson

The first ever in-depth study of one of the world's most enigmatic artists, **Under The Ivy** combines a wealth of new research with rigorous critical scrutiny. Featuring over 70 new interviews with those who have viewed from close quarters both the public artist and the private woman, this compelling biography offers numerous fresh perspectives on a unique and elusive talent.

Under The Ivy examines Bush's unconventional upbringing in south London, the youthful blossoming of her talent and her evolution into one of the most visually and sonically creative artists of the past 35 years. It focuses on her unique working methods and pioneering use of the studio on landmark albums such as *The Dreaming* and *Hounds Of Love*, her rejection of live performance, her key relationships, her profound influence on successive generations of musicians, and the unprecedented spurt of recent activity, resulting in the release of two albums in 2011: the controversial *Director's Cut*, on which Bush reworked 11 songs from her back catalogue, and *50 Words For Snow*, her first album of new material for six years.

The result is a detailed and utterly absorbing biography, written with wit, style and substance.

"The best music biography in perhaps the past decade… magnificent." – The Irish Times
"Superb… a compelling examination of her music." – Mojo
"Respectful, fascinating and full of insight." – Q magazine

Graeme Thomson is the author of several books, including definitive biographies of George Harrison and Elvis Costello. He has written for the *Observer*, *New Statesman*, *Oxford American*, the *Telegraph*, *Time Out* and *Rolling Stone*, and contributes regularly to the *Guardian*, *Uncut*, the *Herald* and *The Arts Desk*.

Available from www.omnibuspress.com

ISBN: 978.1.78038.146.6
Order No: OP54186

TAYLOR SWIFT
THE RISE OF THE NASHVILLE TEEN
By Chlöe Govan

Country pop phenomenon Taylor Swift came from a comfortable Pennsylvania home but set her sights on Nashville early. As a young teenager she won a national poetry competition, wrote her first song and penned a short novel. Perhaps unsurprisingly bullied by her classmates, she was entranced by country music and had already made a series of precocious bids to perform in Music City before her family finally moved there in 2003.

At the age of 14 Taylor Swift became the youngest staff songwriter ever hired by Sony/ATV Tree publishing house. By 2006 her first single had reached the number six slot in *Billboard's* Hot Country Songs chart and after that — and three huge-selling albums —there was no stopping her.

This insightful book about Taylor Swift's short but extraordinary life to date includes the inside story on the high-profile romances that inspired her songs as well as exclusive, in-depth interviews with her childhood friends and early mentors.

Chlöe Govan has written about travel, lifestyle and music for a variety of publications around the world including *Travel Weekly*, the *Times* and *Real Travel*, where she has a monthly column. She is also the author of *Katy Perry: A Life Of Fireworks*, *Rihanna: Rebel Flower* and *Who's Laughing Now: The Jessie J Story*, all published by Omnibus Press.

ISBN: 978.1.78038.354.5
Order No: OP54549